PUFFIN BOOKS

Eyetooth

Frank Rodgers has written and illustrated a wide range of books for children – picture books, story books, non-fiction and novels. His children's stories have been broadcast on radio and TV and he has created a sitcom series for CBBC based on his book *The Intergalactic Kitchen*. His recent work for Puffin includes the *Eyetooth* books and the bestselling *Witch's Dog* and *Robodog* titles. He was an art teacher before becoming an author and illustrator and lives in Glasgow with his wife. He has two grown-up children.

Books by Frank Rodgers

For younger readers

THE WITCH'S DOG
THE WITCH'S DOG AT THE SCHOOL OF SPELLS
THE WITCH'S DOG AND THE MAGIC CAKE
THE WITCH'S DOG AND THE CRYSTAL BALL
THE WITCH'S DOG AND THE FLYING CARPET
THE WITCH'S DOG AND THE ICE-CREAM WIZARD

THE ROBODOG
THE ROBODOG AND THE BIG DIG
THE ROBODOG, SUPERHERO

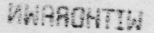

Frank Rodgers

EYETOOTH

PUFFIN

PUFFIN BOOKS

Published by the Penguin Group
Penguin Books Ltd, 80 Strand, London WC2R 0RL, England
Penguin Putnam Inc., 375 Hudson Street, New York, New York 10014, USA
Penguin Books Australia Ltd, 250 Camberwell Road, Camberwell, Victoria 3124, Australia
Penguin Books Canada Ltd, 10 Alcorn Avenue, Toronto, Ontario, Canada M4V 3B2
Penguin Books India (P) Ltd, 11 Community Centre, Panchsheel Park, New Delhi – 110 017, India
Penguin Books (NZ) Ltd, Cnr Rosedale and Airborne Roads, Albany, Auckland, New Zealand
Penguin Books (South Africa) (Pty) Ltd, 24 Sturdee Avenue, Rosebank 2196, South Africa

Penguin Books Ltd, Registered Offices: 80 Strand, London WC2R 0RL, England

www.penguin.com

First published 2003
4

Text copyright © Frank Rodgers, 2003
Illustrations copyright © Chris Inns, 2003
All rights reserved

The moral right of the author and illustrator has been asserted

Set in 14/16.5 pt Adobe Sabon
Typeset by Rowland Phototypesetting Ltd, Bury St Edmunds, Suffolk
Made and printed in England by Clays Ltd, St Ives plc

British Library Cataloguing in Publication Data
A CIP catalogue record for this book is available from the British Library

ISBN 0–141–31615–2

For Liz

Prologue

There are secret places in the world – places where human beings have never set foot. Places where, if they're smart, human beings *should* never set foot. The ragged summit of a dark mountain, deep in the lonely wilds, is one of those places.

A thousand years ago only one castle stood there. Then, gradually, over the centuries other structures were added – all connected to each other by a network of twisting passages, tunnels, lanes, alleys, staircases and bridges. All the buildings, gatehouses and towers crowded together so closely that they resembled nothing so much as a small town. Looking up from the bottom of the mountain during one of those moments when the clouds round the summit briefly part, it would be almost impossible to spot the roofs and towers because they blend in so well with the great, jagged rocks that surround them.

A secret, secretive place – like its occupants.

Secrets, however, can't be kept forever.

As our story begins, the thick, cloudy veil round one of these towers blows aside momentarily and a face appears at the topmost window. It is a furtive, grey face with red eyes and thin, dark lips. Peering down the mountain into the valley, the red eyes glitter. Far below there is something of interest; a group of people in a grassy field. Through the spyglass he can see them clearly enough. There are six people there: two men, two women, a girl and a boy. Four tents have been pitched beside their estate car and caravan. They seem to be making a film. A camera has been set up and one of the men is pointing it at the other. The man being filmed wears a long, brightly-coloured cloak over black clothes. The watcher's eyes narrow at this, and his thin lips twitch in a faint smile. A ray of bright sunlight suddenly escapes from the overhanging clouds and flicks across the landscape towards the tower. Instinctively the watcher pulls his own black cloak up to protect his face and draws back into the shadows. A moment later the clouds close in once more, the sunbeam disappears and the faded, overcast light returns. He looks down again at the activity in the field and slowly licks his lips, the points of his sharp teeth showing briefly against the dark purple of his tongue. Slowly, the returning mist blots out the landscape from view again, clinging to the stone tower and the mountain peak like an icy breath.

Chapter One

'Fake blood!' called Joe's dad, holding up a set of plastic vampire teeth. 'We need more fake blood for my close-up!'

Joe Price was in the middle of painting a stonework pattern on their old caravan. He looked up and his brown eyes crinkled in a smile. His dad, Vinny, was waving at him from the make-up tent on the other side of the field. Vinny's face was chalk-white, his eyebrows jet-black, his lips purple and his dark hair slicked back with grease. In the watery sunlight he looked ghastly . . . exactly the way he wanted to look.

As well as being the director of the film comedy *Vampires on Holiday*, Vinny was also its star . . . Count Clot. It was a very, very low-budget film, which didn't stretch to hiring *real* actors. The film's budget, in fact, didn't stretch to hiring *anyone*. Joe's mum, Nerys, was not only the writer of *Vampires on Holiday*, she was also the make-up artist. His uncle Bill was the cameraman, his cousin Samantha and he were the sound engineers and set painters, and Granny Roz made the costumes and cooked the meals. Everyone helped to make the props. The only real prop they had was a genuine coffin, which Vinny had bought from a disbanded theatre group. At the moment this was still tied to the roof rack of the car by its brass carrying handles.

The coffin gave Joe the creeps. It made him think about dead things . . . ghosts . . . vampires; especially at night, when he imagined the lid creaking open and a vampire climbing out. Every morning when he woke in his small, one-man tent, he felt his neck just to make sure there were no holes in it. He knew this was silly but he couldn't help it. The fact that his dad's vampire movie was a comedy certainly helped make Joe feel better about it during the day, but it didn't stop his imagination from working overtime at night. Joe hated ghost stories and horror films, and recently one or two kids in his class had found this out and teased him about it. To prove he wasn't a scaredy-cat Joe accepted a dare on the last day of term.

The dare was a creepy one. Joe had to stick his hand into a hole in a tree. Not just any old tree. This one was special. It stood, twisted and scaly, in a fenced-off patch of wild, scrubby ground not far from the school. There was a hole in its trunk that looked like an eye socket in a skull. All the kids called the hole 'the empty eye' and there were plenty of stories about how it could suck you in if you got too close.

Almost the whole class gathered after school to watch Joe do it. Hemmed in by the pressing bodies and eager grins of his classmates, Joe faced up to the tree. His insides felt as hollow as the old trunk. Slowly, he lifted up his hand and edged it towards the hole. He felt his heart starting to pound and his mouth becoming dry. Somehow he managed to stop himself from trembling. His hand reached nearer and nearer.

'Do it! Do it!' urged his classmates.

But Joe couldn't do it. He pulled his hand away and turned his back on the tree.

'Scaredy-cat!' the jostling kids taunted as Joe retreated and made his miserable way home. 'Scaredy-cat! Scaredy-cat!'

So, Joe's summer holidays had started badly. The word 'scaredy-cat' went round and round in his head, repeating like a stuck CD.

Luckily he had been able to push it to the back of his mind on the film set. Being with his family gave Joe the chance to forget his troubles at school. He enjoyed mucking in and had actually helped write the next scene, in which Count Clot arrived at a vampire holiday camp in his travelling castle.

'Fake blood, Joe!' Vinny called again, breaking into Joe's thoughts.

Joe put down his paintbrush and lifted up an empty container.

'There's no fake blood left, Dad. Mum used it all on the dancing werewolves yesterday.' The dancing werewolves had been played by four members of the local amateur dramatic club. They hadn't been very good, but at least they hadn't cost anything.

Vinny's face fell, then immediately brightened again as he spotted a bottle of tomato ketchup on the picnic table near the car.

'No probs!' he cried. 'I'll use that.' Hurrying across the grass, his flowery Count Clot 'beachwear' cape flapping, Vinny snatched up the bottle.

Joe smiled. His dad was an incredible optimist – convinced he'd be a top Hollywood director one day. Vinny was full of crazy, over-the-top film ideas that never quite worked out. Each summer for the last couple of years, instead of having a family holiday, Joe's dad had tried to make a film. Two years ago it had been *Hamsters from Mars*, a drama about an alien vet. Last year it was *Bounced Out*, the sad tale of an ageing acrobat. The big idea this year was a vampire comedy.

'Hollywood will love it!' Vinny had cried, bursting with his habitual enthusiasm.

Hollywood, of course, couldn't have cared less and told him so. But Vinny was unstoppable. He had managed to get a little money together, roped in his family again as the film crew and set off for the mountains.

Joe's mum was as enthusiastic as Vinny. 'Third time lucky!' she had said as they set out in their old estate car.

So here they were, in a small field rented from a local farmer. The field lay at the edge of a forest which swept in an impenetrable mass up the side of a dark mountain, whose top was almost continually wreathed in mist. 'Deep in the heart of the middle of nowhere,' as his mum had put it.

'Ah yes, feel the atmosphere!' Vinny had replied. 'Atmosphere! This is the land of vampires if I'm not mistaken. And if it isn't, then it should be! The perfect place to make a vampire comedy. Wouldn't it be just great if we bumped into one? We could ask him to be in the movie, ha ha!' Chuckling to himself, he had stuck a notice on the fence by the side of the road.

VAMPIRES WANTED
(Must have own fangs.) Ask for Vinny.

A week later the sign was still there, tattered and spattered with mud from the farmer's tractor. So far it had attracted no vampires.

That evening, the painting and filming

over for the day, Joe sat on the fence peeling a banana. As he took his first bite he heard the tractor not far off, and a few minutes later it came trundling round the bend and stopped in front of him. Its headlights caught the sign as it approached and the farmer peered through the gloom and read it for the first time.

'Vampires, is it, Joe?' he chortled, leaning on the steering wheel and pushing his cap to the back of his bald head. 'Why don't you go up to Eyetooth and knock on a few doors? You're sure to find plenty!' He chuckled again. 'If you can get up there, that is. There's no road and there's an almost sheer cliff all the way round.'

'Eyetooth?' asked Joe. 'Where's that?'

The farmer pointed to the mountain, its top shrouded in a swirling mist that seemed to glow like white fire in the cold light of the new moon.

'There,' he said, winking. 'They do say there's a vampire village up there, with castles and all. Can't say I believe it myself, mind you.'

Joe stared at the mountain and felt the hairs on the back of his neck prickle with the familiar feeling of fear. Telling himself not to be such a wimp, he screwed up his eyes for a better look. As he did so, the wreaths of mist parted, revealing the dark, jutting points of the summit outlined harshly in the cold moonlight.

'I suppose those could be pointed roofs,' he said, trying not to sound nervous. 'Hard to tell.'

'They could be,' replied the farmer. 'But I don't think they are. And anyway, who in their right mind would want to go up there and find out, eh?'

'Not me,' answered Joe fervently.

After the farmer left, Joe sat and gazed up at the sky. Dark, streaming clouds raced past the bright moon like the ragged banners of a ghostly army. A perfect night for vampires, he thought, and gave a little involuntary shiver, pulling up the hood of his sweatshirt. He lowered his eyes to the mountain top and blinked, his heart suddenly thumping. Was it his imagination again or could he see little pin-pricks of light winking among the crags? As he stared, the mist descended, swirling and drifting, and once more the summit of the mountain was obscured. Joe shook his head. Surely no one could be up there? No, he thought. What he had seen was probably just the glint of moonlight on the rocks. Probably.

For a moment, though . . . just for a moment . . . he thought he'd seen the lighted windows of a castle.

Chapter Two

Along the wall glided the black shape of a vampire. Silently it crept across the dark room until it was right behind the figure in the chair. Spreading its cloak out like a black shroud, the vampire opened its mouth and slowly bent its head down towards the figure's neck.

Then it stopped and stood upright.

'It's no use,' said the vampire. 'I can't do it. I just can't bite a neck – even though I know it's only pretend. Sorry.'

At once a torch flared and the vampire stood blinking in the glare. The gloomy room was revealed as a study, with leather-bound books on shelves, astrological charts on the wall and a frowning inquisitor, Countess Alchema, seated at her desk. A large torch, burning brightly in its wrought-iron stand, stood beside her, its light gleaming on her upswept silver hair and softening the hard angles of her white face. She tapped the end of her quill impatiently on the desk.

'For goodness' sake, Count Moonsley,' she said. 'You're a vampire. You're *supposed* to bite necks. It's what vampires *do*!'

Count Moonsley spread his hands and grinned wryly. He was a young vampire with a cheerful face and a shock of spiky orange hair.

'Not this vampire, I'm afraid,' he said. 'My teeth just refuse to sink into a neck . . . even a fake one covered in rat's blood.' He patted the dummy figure that sat by the window, shaking his head disapprovingly at the dark redness glistening on the neck and shoulders. 'What is all this about? Count Fibula's only been leader of the council for a few days, and already he's got Eyetooth in an uproar by insisting on some of us coming up here to be tested in our vampire skills. Why can't he just leave things as they are?'

Alchema glowered. 'Fibula doesn't like

things the way they are. He thinks things were better in the past.'

'That's his opinion. As for me, I'm happy . . . and so are my friends.'

'Fibula thinks that we have become lazy, up here in our safe haven of Eyetooth.'

'But that's the point of Eyetooth,' protested Count Moonsley. 'We're all up here because over the centuries we were hunted nearly to extinction by vampire-killers with their wooden stakes and silver bullets. This is the last refuge of the vampires. We all like the idea that no one knows about us.'

'But that secrecy comes at a price, Count Moonsley,' said Alchema. 'It means that for the last half-century or so, no vampire has risked going down the mountain in search of human blood.'

'They don't have to,' said Moonsley. 'Everyone exists on rat's blood now.'

'Everyone except you,' said Alchema darkly. 'You don't drink blood at all.'

'It's no secret,' said Moonsley amiably. 'I get my vitamins in other ways . . . from fruit and vegetables. I've even got my own vegetable patch. These days I prefer to sink my teeth into a tomato instead of a rat.

I find that fruit and veg make me feel good.'

'Vampires aren't meant to feel good,' retorted Countess Alchema. 'They're meant to feel like death warmed up. Vampires might change if they don't have blood. That's what many are afraid of.' She peered at him intently. '*You* might change.'

Moonsley grinned. 'Vampires shouldn't be afraid of change,' he replied. 'Time they joined the twenty-first century.'

The countess shook her head again and gazed at the young vampire through narrowed eyes. 'You do realize what you're being called because of this, don't you, Count Moonsley?' She continued to stare meaningfully at him. 'Count "Muesli". Muesli! That mixture of grit and birdseed which the outsiders call health food. Don't you find that embarrassing?'

Count Moonsley grinned.

'Not at all,' he replied. 'What's in a name? Anyway, I like it. All my friends call me Muesli now.'

The countess was astonished. 'They do?' She shook her head as she took it in. 'And you don't mind?'

'Of course not! In fact,' he went on, his eyes twinkling, 'we've known each other

17

for a long time, Countess, so why don't you call me Muesli, too. I'd like that.'

'Very well,' she replied slowly. 'If you insist, Count . . . *Muesli*.'

'There you are,' replied the count with a smile. 'Wasn't too bad, was it?'

Despite herself, the countess laughed then shook her head, becoming serious again. 'You're a bad influence, you know,' said Alchema.

'Am I?' said Muesli, startled. 'Says who?'

'Fibula,' replied the teacher. 'He says there are quite a few vampires who are thinking of following your lead and giving up blood. That's why he arranged these tests and put you first in line. He wants to "weed out" all those vampires who are losing their taste for the red nectar.'

'"Weed out"? What do you mean?'

'Exactly what it sounds like,' said Alchema. 'Fibula has ordered that, if anyone fails the tests, then they are to be sent packing. Banished from Eyetooth.'

Count Muesli stared at her in amazement.

'Surely not!' he said. 'I thought all this was just about shaking everyone up a bit. Surely he can't mean it?'

Alchema sighed. 'He means it, all right,' she replied. Reaching across the table, she picked up a sheaf of ancient paper and looked at it, shaking her head. 'I've checked the constitution of the Eyetooth Council and it seems that the leader has the power to banish a vampire for . . . quote . . . *failure to meet vampire standards* . . . unquote. So, you have to pass this test or . . .' She shrugged and grimaced again. 'I have to say, in confidence, Muesli, that I don't like this one bit, and I'm going to do my best to make sure no one fails. The little bit of power he has as leader of the council has probably gone to his head. Hopefully, all this will blow over.'

Muesli looked at the stern face of the old countess and didn't reply for a moment. 'So . . . did I pass?' he asked softly.

'Let's see,' she said and looked down at her notes.

Count Muesli glanced at the books on the shelves behind her, waiting for her to come to a decision. He ran his fingers along the leather-bound spines. All the great vampire books were here: *Great Indentations* . . . *The Bloodsucker's Who's Who* . . . *Doom, Gloom and Tomb* . . . *Red Fang* . . .

but he couldn't concentrate for thinking about the result of the test. Surely Alchema wouldn't fail him?

'Hmmm,' said Countess Alchema at last. 'You've just failed *Neck-biting Techniques* but you did very well indeed on *Scare Tactics* and *Mind Control* . . . your hypnotic chant and vampire scream were most impressive . . . as was your *Vampire History* . . .' She looked up and fixed Muesli with a thoughtful gaze. 'You are supposed to be successful in all the disciplines tested and, as such, should fail . . . but –' the countess frowned, suddenly angry – 'as I regard these tests as meaningless anyway, I believe you have done enough to pass.'

Muesli beamed. 'Thank you, Countess!' he cried, then his smile faded. 'But I don't want to get you into any trouble.'

Shrugging, the countess smiled. 'Don't worry about me, Muesli. I'm a wily old vixen . . . older and wiser than Fibula.'

'Well,' said Muesli, his usual carefree attitude quickly returning, 'I'm relieved.'

Alchema opened her desk and pulled out a roll of parchment. Spreading it out on the desktop, she put a little gargoyle paperweight on each of the corners, dipped her quill in the inkwell and began to write. It didn't take long, and a few minutes later she was finished. She signed it at the bottom, blotted it and handed it to Count Muesli. 'You'll have to get Fibula's signature on this. You'll find him at his castle.'

'Thank you, Countess Alchema,' said Count Muesli. 'I'm glad this is over. Now I can get back to enjoying myself. I might take my coffincar out for a spin.'

The countess sighed. 'Another of your innovations, Muesli,' she said. 'Mobile coffins. The most unlikely vampires have them now.'

Count Muesli grinned. 'My coffincar is a beauty – bright yellow. I've had it out in the mountain tunnels and forest roads. It travels.'

The countess sniffed. 'I may be a bit old-fashioned, Muesli, but I think that the only vampire transport should be a black, horse-drawn hearse with black plumes and black tassels.'

'Yellow's the new black,' said Count Muesli. 'Anyway, coffincars are easier to look after than horse-drawn hearses . . . and a lot more fun.'

Countess Alchema shook her head.

'Fun,' she muttered darkly. 'It's sure to lead to trouble.'

Chapter Three

'Corpy!' Muesli called. 'Corpy! Are you there?'

There was no answer, so he tried again.

'Corpy!'

From out of the arched cloister at the far end of the courtyard, the figure of a big vampire appeared. He hurried across the ancient flagstones towards Count Muesli, his cloak billowing, his hair wild.

Count Corpus – or 'Corpuscles the Muscles', as he was known to his friends – was built like a boulder and, as well as being Eyetooth's only policeman, he was Count Muesli's best friend.

'Sorry, I'm late, Mooz,' he said as he ran

up. 'Been investigating a robbery. A crystal decanter containing Countess Plaza's last remaining drops of human blood has disappeared.' He stopped to catch his breath, mopping his brow with the end of his cloak. 'She's very angry. The blood was kept fresh by a secret process. She says she was saving it for a special occasion. It's a serious business.'

'It certainly is,' replied Count Muesli. 'Who would do a thing like that? It would mean exile from Eyetooth.'

'Exactly,' said Count Corpus. Suddenly he blinked and smacked his forehead. 'What am I thinking of?' he cried. 'Here am I, going on about work, and I forgot to ask about you! How did it go with Alchema?' He jerked his thumb upwards in the direction of the study in the tower. 'Did you pass?'

Count Muesli pulled out the rolled-up parchment and waved it in the air. 'I did!'

'Great!' cried Corpus. 'Let's celebrate. A glass or two of fizzy Fangola at the Café in the Crypt.'

They began to stroll back across the courtyard.

'I must say this whole "tests" thing is

an annoyance,' Corpus said. 'Krazul and Darceth are due to be tested tomorrow, and they are not looking forward to it.' He glanced at Muesli. 'They'll pass, won't they?'

'Of course they will,' Muesli reassured him. 'Our friends will be fine, you'll see.'

'What would have happened if you had failed?' asked Corpus. 'Did Alchema say?'

Count Muesli made a face. 'Kicked out of Eyetooth, no less,' he said.

'What?' spluttered Corpus, stopping in his tracks. 'That's ridiculous. The countess must have made a mistake surely?'

'No, she was sure,' Muesli replied. 'But anyway, it's nothing,' he went on, waving a hand airily. 'Forget it. Countess Alchema thinks that becoming leader has gone to Fibula's head. She feels this will all blow over soon.'

'But what . . .?' Corpus began again.

'Let's not worry about it,' Muesli said lightly. He smiled up at his big friend. 'Relax. I passed, didn't I? It's time to celebrate.'

The big vampire grinned, and they set off again.

'You're right,' he said. 'Eyetooth will be back to normal in no time. Let's go get that glass of Fangola!'

Chapter Four

The soft night wind sighed around the tent, rustling the leaves in the big trees that bordered the field. Joe zipped up his sleeping bag, propped himself on one elbow and adjusted the lamp hanging above him. Feeling inside his rucksack, he found his book and pulled it out. As he settled down to read he glanced at the cover and gave another involuntary shiver.

'Oh no,' he muttered. '*The Undead Centre: Ten Chilling Vampire Tales*. I picked up Dad's book by mistake. That's all I need. I meant to bring *The Mega Joke Annual*.' He shoved the book back in his rucksack, switched off the lamp and lay back with his arms behind his head. The left side of his tent was in darkness but the right was softly and reassuringly lit by the light streaming from the caravan's window. Mum, Dad, Bill and Granny Roz were in there, playing cards. Joe sighed. He enjoyed the trips with his film-mad mum and dad, but he also knew that this one would probably be the last. Granny Roz, Samantha and Bill had been muttering that unless *Vampires on Holiday* was a success, they would not be helping again. Oh well, thought Joe, next year it'll be back to normal summer holidays for me. A week in a theme park or two weeks in Benidorm. He wasn't looking forward to it. Joe preferred being on his own somewhere quiet. He really liked messing about, making movies with the family. The thought of not having the films to look forward to made Joe feel depressed. Then the dreaded word 'scaredy-cat' bobbed to the surface of his mind again and he had to concentrate to make it sink.

He burrowed further down into his sleeping bag and turned on to his side, away from the light. No sooner had he shut his eyes than a noise outside made them fly open again. Holding his breath, he listened, wondering what it could be. Faint sounds of merriment drifted from the caravan and he could hear his mum's high, giggling laughter, but this noise was coming from just outside the tent. Turning slowly towards the light, he levered himself up into a sitting position. Then he froze. A shadow was moving slowly across the right-hand side of his tent. The shadow of a figure wearing a high collar, its hands held up in front of its face with the fingers spread out like claws. It was the unmistakable shape of a vam-pire. A sudden coldness pricked the back of Joe's neck and he felt his heart start to pound. Was the farmer's story about Eyetooth true? Were there really vampires in the mountains? Was this one of them?

Joe's imagination was now roaring ahead on full throttle. His heart was pounding so much now, it felt like it was going to jump out of his chest. Without taking his eyes off the shadow, he groped around beside his rucksack with a shaky hand until his fingers closed on his heavy rubber-coated torch. Lifting it up like a club, he unzipped the sleeping bag. He sat there, rigid, wondering what to do, when suddenly the figure tripped, stumbled and fell.

'For crying out loud!' muttered a familiar voice. 'Who left that there?'

'Dad?' Joe gasped, getting out of his sleeping bag. 'Is that you?'

'Sorry to wake you, Joe,' his dad's voice came back. 'Tripped over a paint pot.'

All Joe's fears evaporated. He pulled on a jersey, slipped his feet into his trainers and unzipped the tent.

His dad, in full Count Clot costume, was sitting on the ground, one shoe off, rubbing his toes. Beside him stood the camera on its tripod, the red light glowing.

'Have you been . . . filming?' Joe asked in surprise.

'I didn't want to bother the others so I thought I'd get a few shots of the count creeping around in the dark.'

Joe went over to the camera and switched it off. He peered through the viewfinder.

'Can't see much, Dad. It's too dark to film.'

Vinny sighed, put his shoe back on and got up. His long face seemed even longer.

'Too bad,' he said, then flashed Joe his usual good-natured smile. 'I thought I'd try and push the movie along a bit. We're quite a way behind schedule.'

'Things not going too well then, Dad?' asked Joe, already feeling that *Vampires on Holiday* was destined to be another failure.

'Never say die,' replied Vinny with a cheerful grin. 'At least,' he winked and nudged Joe with his elbow, 'that's what the vampires say, eh?'

'None of them answered your advert,' said Joe, smiling, as he helped his dad pack the camera away. He was pleased to be joking about vampires instead of being attacked by one.

'Advert? Which advert?' Vinny was puzzled.

'The one on the fence,' replied Joe. 'You know . . . *Vampires Wanted . . .*?'

'Oh, that!' exclaimed his dad, grinning. 'Yeah, it is a pity. I could certainly do with a real, live bloodsucker to play the baddie in the film. But I really don't think one is going to come wandering along that lane to knock on our door, do you?'

'No,' said Joe. 'I don't suppose I do.' I certainly hope not, anyway, he thought.

Vinny put the camera in the boot of the car and turned back towards the caravan. 'Goodnight, then, Joe.'

Joe stifled a yawn. 'Goodnight, Clot. I mean . . . Dad.'

He heard his dad's chuckle as he got back into his tent. Sliding into his warm sleeping bag again, he sighed and closed his eyes. A minute later he was fast asleep.

Chapter Five

The night wind was colder up on the mountain and its sighs were harsher.

Count Fibula listened for a moment as it gusted eerily around the battlements. His red eyes glittered and the ghost of a smile hovered around his thin, dark lips. He turned away abruptly from the narrow window, his cloak swinging out behind him like a black flag.

'It begins,' he murmured, rubbing his hands with satisfaction. 'The process which will rid Eyetooth of all its dead weight. They will go and perish in the outside world. Those who remain here will be the strong, trustworthy ones . . . the ones who will not be afraid to take their rightful places in the world again. Once more, vampires will strike fear into every human heart . . . and I will be their ruler!' His lips twitched as they again attempted to stretch into a smile. He glared at Ichor, his squat servant, who was standing near the ornate carved fireplace, rubbing his hands in a fair imitation of his master. 'Beginning with Moonsley, they'll all be ejected from Eyetooth soon.' Fibula began to pace up and down in front of the fire. 'Moonsley . . .' he muttered, shaking his head. 'With every other vampire I know what I'm dealing with, but with Moonsley it's unclear. He may well just be a silly, empty-headed, *fun-loving* young vampire with no thoughts except for himself, but there are too many vampires here who think of following his example.'

Ichor sidled up to his master and copied his smirk. 'It's disgusting, Master,' he said. 'Imagine . . . a vampire who doesn't like the taste of blood.' He snorted in disdain. 'A *veggie* vampire. It isn't natural! And who knows . . . it might be infectious. They call him "Muesli", you know, Master.'

Fibula snorted. 'Ha! A fitting name for a bloodless creature!'

'What I can't understand,' said Ichor, 'is why "Muesli" is so popular with some of the vampires.'

Fibula thrust his face at Ichor, his dark-red eyes blazing. Ichor backed off towards the fireplace, feeling the heat of the burning logs on his considerable backside.

'Being popular means nothing!' Fibula snarled. 'Nothing! It's power that counts. When you have power, you can do anything you like.' His expression became cold. 'When I have complete power here, anyone who so much as contradicts me will be thrown into my dungeons.'

'Er ... we don't have any dungeons,' said Ichor in a small voice, edging away from the heat.

'Then we'll build some!' cried Fibula. 'What's the use of a castle without dungeons?'

'You have the west tower room,' Ichor suggested hesitantly. 'That's been used as a prison before. It even has a booby trap to protect it.'

Fibula snorted. 'Not the same. There have to be dungeons. All the other castles have dungeons. And that's another thing ... their dungeons are full of rats. It means they have their own supply. I have to buy them in.' He stalked across the floor and flopped into a throne-like chair at the head of his great table. 'Rats,' he snarled, glaring balefully at his servant. 'That's how low we've become. Feeding on animals. We're almost as bad as humans.' Fibula's eyes took on a faraway look. 'Humans,' he murmured. 'Ahhh yes. I can't remember when I last sank my teeth into a plump human neck. We've skulked about up here for the last few centuries, hiding in our castles, afraid of the vampire-hunters. Well, no more. Now that I am leader, things will change.'

Ichor nodded eagerly. 'For the better, Master.'

Fibula's eyes glittered. 'Yes. Before long the great days will return when vampires stalk the land and humans are afraid to go out after dark. My castle will be the centre of a new vampire empire!' His dreamy look vanished and he sniffed. 'Castle!' he said sullenly, suddenly remembering one of the things that irked him. 'What's the use of a castle without servants? I've only got you. Which reminds me of something I saw today,' he murmured, a sudden gleam flickering in his red eyes. 'A possible answer to my little servant problem.' He licked his lips greedily.

Just then the doorbell jangled.

Fibula sank deeper into his chair as Ichor hurried from the room. Fibula heard the creaking and groaning of the great outer door of the castle as it was unlocked and opened, then there was a short silence, followed by the murmur of voices.

Ichor's head appeared round the door. He was blinking nervously.

'It ... it's ... Moo ... Moo ...' he stammered.

'Why are you standing there doing cow impressions?' shouted Count Fibula in annoyance. 'Show them in!'

Ichor's head disappeared, the door opened wide and into the room walked Count Muesli and Count Corpus.

Fibula stiffened and clutched the edge of the table in surprise.

'Come to say goodbye, "Muesli"?' he snarled.

Count Muesli's eyes swept round the huge, vaulted hall before he answered. He had never been in Fibula's castle before and he was surprised to see how grand it was –

despite the grime of decades. Blood-red, dusty velvet drapes covered the tall windows, an enormous, soot-blackened stone fireplace encrusted with hideous gargoyles rose to the ceiling, and a heavy, cobwebbed candelabra hung overhead.

'No, Count Fibula,' he replied at last, holding out the parchment. 'Countess Alchema has given me a pass mark. All it needs is your signature. I brought Count Corpus along to witness it.'

Count Fibula's mouth was opening and closing soundlessly, like a fish, so he closed it tight and stared in disbelief.

'You . . . *passed*?' he hissed at last, and Muesli grinned.

'I did. Isn't that nice?'

'Just the ticket,' Corpus said, grinning.

Count Fibula ground his teeth in frustration. He knew he had to sign the parchment. The vampires would find out that Muesli had passed and would turn on him if he didn't sign. The undead of Eyetooth had a very strong sense of justice. He had been certain that Muesli would fail, so what had gone wrong? *Alchema*, he thought. Yes. Alchema must be to blame. She hadn't done her job properly. And who

38

knows . . . she might even be in league with Muesli. He would have to deal with Alchema.

Ichor scurried round behind Count Fibula's chair and, leaning over, whispered in his master's ear. 'Signing will make you popular, Master,' he hissed quietly. 'Remember we always have *Plan B*!'

Fibula nodded slowly, then looked at Count Muesli. 'Well . . . done, Muesli,' he said with an effort. 'Well . . . done.'

'Thank you,' replied Muesli, beaming.

Fibula took the offered parchment and laid it on the table in front of him, looking down to conceal the sudden smirk on his face. He reached across to the bat-shaped writing stand and plucked a quill from the pen holder. Dipping it in an inkwell of bat's blood, he quickly signed his name across the bottom.

Corpus moved to his side and took the pen from his hand. 'My turn,' he said and signed his own name as witness. Picking up the parchment, he waved it in the air until it was dry, rolled it up and stuffed it into an inside pocket. 'As constable of Eyetooth I'll take charge of this,' he said importantly.

'Thank you, Count Fibula,' said Count Muesli politely. 'Count Corpus and I will be leaving now.' With a nod to Ichor, who had trotted over to open the door, he and Corpus left, banging the great outer door behind them.

Fibula stood up slowly, then suddenly reached out, took hold of a heavy candlestick and hurled it at the wall. It hit the stonework with a glancing blow, striking sparks, then fell to the floor with a dull clang. Fibula turned to Ichor, his red eyes glittering. 'Why am I so worried about that nobody?' He shook his head. 'Never mind. I'll soon be rid of him. He nodded at his servant and smiled evilly. '*Plan B*, then. You know what to do?'

'I do, Master, I do,' Ichor murmured eagerly, giving quick little bows as he backed away. 'I do indeed.' Rubbing his hands gleefully, he turned and scuttled out.

Chapter Six

The wind had died down and the campsite was quiet now. Everyone had gone to bed. The only night sounds to be heard were the occasional soft hoot of an owl and little flurries of snores from the caravan.

Joe was dreaming he was at the Oscars ceremony in Hollywood. His mum and dad, Granny Roz, Samantha and Bill were there too. *Vampires on Holiday* had been nominated for Best Film! Not only that, Vinny had been nominated for Best Director, Nerys for Best Writer, Bill for Best Cameraman, Samantha for Best Sound and Granny Roz for Best Costumes. Joe had been nominated for Best Actor, which, even in his dream, puzzled him since he knew he hadn't been in the film.

The stage set for the Oscars was a gigantic sandcastle, with towers, turrets and battlements, and the stage itself looked just like a beach. On the beach, four werewolves in brightly-coloured beachwear were performing a dance routine. A famous actress wearing a paint pot on her head arrived on a tractor and, as the werewolves danced around the tractor, she climbed off and stepped up to the microphone. There was a burst of applause as she held up a golden envelope and ripped it open. The audience held its breath. Suddenly, without knowing how they got there, Joe found that he and his family were on stage and the werewolves were presenting them with their Oscars. They had all won! Beside him he heard his mum's bubbly laughter and Bill's deep chortle. There was another burst of applause.

Vinny held up his hand and everyone fell silent.

'I always dreamed I'd win an Oscar one day,' he said, 'but I didn't really believe my dream would come true.' The audience applauded. 'I'd like to thank my family . . .'

That's as far as Vinny got. With a blood-curdling scream that nearly woke Joe up, a vampire ran on to the stage. His face was white, his lips were purple, his red eyes were blazing and a flowery cape flapped and cracked behind him. Joe saw at once it was Count Clot, the funny vampire that his dad had played in the film. But one look at the angry white face told him that this Count Clot did not have a sense of humour. He was a real vampire and was deadly serious. Joe couldn't move. Fear gripped him and he felt ashamed.

Count Clot stopped and pointed at Joe's dad. 'You made fun of me!' he cried. 'I have come for revenge!'

Before anyone could react, the vampire grabbed Vinny and sank its fangs into his neck. Joe gasped in horror and heard himself shout, 'Dad!'

The audience applauded again as Vinny became a vampire too . . . another identical Count Clot. Both vampires now turned towards the family, fingers twitching. The audience clapped yet again and began to cheer. Joe realized they thought that this was part of the entertainment. Desperately he shouted to them for help, but they just clapped and cheered even more.

Joe's happy dream had become a nightmare. Frantically he looked around. What could he do? The rest of the family seemed to be frozen with fear too – they stood staring at the advancing vampires, eyes wide and mouths open. Joe looked down at the Oscar he was holding. Suddenly he realized that if he could get close enough to the vampires, he could use his Oscar like a magic wand. But was he brave enough? He closed his eyes. Yes, he told himself. I can be. I *have* to be.

Taking a deep breath, he walked towards the vampires, holding the Oscar in front of him. The two vampires stood still and watched him coming, their eyes narrowed and little smiles on their dark lips. Joe could tell that they believed he was walking to his doom. But still he approached them, terrified and defiant at the same time. All he knew was, he had to save his father and his family. As he got close, both vampires suddenly hissed and lunged towards him, mouths wide and fangs bared. Shocked, Joe wanted to turn and run, but he didn't. He stood his ground and pointed the Oscar at them.

With a flash like a bursting firework, a bolt of light shot from the end of the Oscar and hit the two vampires. For a second they glowed, white-hot, then were transformed. Vampire Dad became Dad again and Count Clot turned into a big banana. Applause. At once the werewolves presented the banana with a special Oscar for Best Piece of Fruit. More applause. Then a famous producer ran on to the stage and offered the banana a starring role in his next movie.

The audience were now cheering wildly. From the wings, photographers crowded on to the stage to take everyone's photograph.

Vinny was ecstatic. He jumped up and down, waving his Oscar in the air and yelling, 'I'm the Count of Hollywood!'

Joe stood next to his dad and, as they both held up their Oscars for the cameras, Joe realized that his Oscar wasn't an Oscar any more. It was a postcard from Benidorm.

Vinny bent down and whispered in his ear. 'That's where we'll be going on holiday from now on, Joe,' he said. 'No more filming. No more filming . . .'

The dream faded into nothing. With a sigh and a feeling of intense disappointment, Joe turned over in his sleep.

Chapter Seven

Muesli and Corpus descended into the twilight gloom of the Café in the Crypt, a favourite vampire meeting place for hundreds of years. Although vampires usually preferred being alone, there were times when they liked the company of other vampires. When they did, they often came to the Café in the Crypt for a cup of strong, bitter coffee or a raw ratburger. Sometimes, the vampires came just to sit in one of the dark alcoves and listen to the ancient brass coffee machine as it hissed and spluttered while they dreamed of past glories; of blood and badness.

As the two friends came down the curving stairway, it became obvious that everyone here knew the result of the test.

'So you'll be staying,' gurgled old Count Zircon, sinking his yellow fangs into a ratburger. 'Mmmm . . . interesting.'

'Yes, well done, Muesli,' added Countess Bray in her loud voice, patting him on the shoulder as he and Corpus stepped up to the café counter. 'Well done, indeed. Testing is a silly idea, and banishment for failing is an even sillier one!'

Countess Bray was as bloodthirsty a vampire as any in Eyetooth, but she hated Count Fibula. She was in favour of anyone who ruffled his feathers.

Muesli smiled. He liked Bray. Straight-forward and honest, she always looked as if she had just got out of her coffin. Her greenish curls were tousled and her cloak was crumpled and creased. There were also a few oily smudges on her pale, round face.

'Been tinkering with my old mobile resting place again, Muesli,' she boomed. 'Can't get it to run, I'm afraid.'

Count Muesli smiled happily. 'I'll come round and have a look at your coffin-car if you like, Countess. The problem will probably be in the self-winding spring mechanism.'

'Splendid!' cried Countess Bray. 'Splendid! It's selfish, I know, but I'm very glad you're still around!'

Grume, the one-legged owner of the café, nodded as he wiped two glasses and placed them on the oak counter in front of Muesli and Corpus.

'It's good news for me,' he said in his low, gravelly voice. He limped over to a shelf, his wooden leg thumping dully on the flagstones. Coming back with a dark-green bottle of Fangola, he filled up the glasses. 'Means I won't lose a customer.'

'How did you all find out I had passed the test?' asked Count Muesli.

Grume inclined his head towards a table in the corner and smirked. 'A little bat told us,' he said.

Muesli looked round and saw Countess Alchema sitting by one of the marble tombs that served as tables.

She glanced up and raised her glass of Fangola to him. 'No problem with Fibula, I take it?' she asked, her eyes glinting.

'Not really,' replied Count Muesli with a smile. 'Although I could tell he wasn't too pleased.'

There was a sudden scraping of chairs on

the stone floor and two hooded vampires, one short and one tall, emerged from a dim alcove in the opposite corner. They pushed past Muesli and Corpus roughly, jostling their elbows so that they nearly dropped their glasses. One of them hissed, 'No, and there are some *here* who aren't too pleased neither.'

'Very *un*-pleased,' muttered the other.

Count Muesli thought he recognized the voices but he couldn't place them. Nor could he see their faces, hidden as they were deep in the hoods. He was about to ask them what they meant, but the two vampires quickly climbed the stairs, their long, grimy cloaks trailing on the dusty steps.

The door banged behind them and Corpus glanced at his friend. 'They don't seem to like you, Mooz,' he said.

Count Muesli grinned cheerily. 'Who cares?' he replied. 'I don't know them and I don't really want to.'

Corpus smiled and took a sip of Fangola. 'You're right,' he said. 'This is a lot of fuss over nothing.'

'Although,' Alchema murmured, 'I have a feeling that those two are friends of Fibula. Just the types to get nasty, given half a chance. I'd keep an eye on them if I were you, Count Muesli.'

Corpus smiled and patted himself on the chest importantly. 'Don't worry, Countess. I'm the policeman around here. I'll watch out for them.'

'Thanks, Corpy,' said Muesli with a grin. 'But I wasn't really worried in the first place.'

Corpus shrugged, took another drink and smiled. 'Ahh!' he said in satisfaction as he licked his lips. 'Fangola! Nothing like it. The drink that vampires like best – after the red nectar, of course. Rainwater filtered through a graveyard, crushed toadstools, deadly nightshade, hellebore, devil's club, baneberry and recently a *secret* ingredient.' He flashed a quick, meaningful glance at Grume. 'Whatever you've added to the original recipe, Grume, it's a winner!'

'I heartily agree!' cried Countess Alchema, licking her lips too as she put down her glass on the marble tomb. 'It has a delightfully sharp taste. Perhaps one day you'll let us into the secret, Grume?'

Grume shrugged and continued to wipe the counter top.

*

Corpus and Muesli had been chatting for a few minutes when the door of the Café in the Crypt high above them opened and in came Vane, Corpus's assistant. Vane was a werewolf who hated getting wet so much, he put up his umbrella every time he went out of doors.

'What are you doing here, Vane?' asked Corpus mildly. 'Aren't you supposed to be looking after the office?'

The little werewolf hurried down the steps, furling his still-dry umbrella. He looked up at his boss and nodded with some agitation. 'I was,' he said. 'But then these fellers came in and said they had important news . . . evidence, like . . . about Countess Plaza's missing decanter. Asked for you. They're waiting. Down at the office,' he added unnecessarily.

'Oh? Right,' said Corpus briskly. 'I'll see to it immediately.' He turned, picked up his glass of Fangola and took a sip. 'Nip back to the office, will you? Tell them I'll be there directly.'

Vane nodded. 'I will,' he said briskly. At the top of the stairs he opened the door and looked out. The night was still dry, but Vane unfurled his umbrella anyway. He stepped across the threshold, but his brolly was too big to go through the door behind him. The little werewolf jerked at the handle impatiently, trying to free it. From downstairs in the café it looked as if a giant bat was trying to shoulder its way in. Finally Vane yanked the brolly clear, pulled the door shut and hurried away up the alley, the increasingly tattered umbrella held low over his head.

Corpus drained his glass of Fangola and turned to Muesli. 'Duty calls, I'm afraid, Mooz. Have to go.'

Count Muesli smiled. 'See you later, Corpy,' he said. 'I'm going home in a moment anyway. My coffincar needs a wash. It's all muddy from the mountain roads.' He laughed. 'The way it looks now, I wouldn't be seen dead in it.'

Chapter Eight

Half an hour later, Count Muesli had just finished washing his coffincar. It was parked in the courtyard entrance to his small, castellated house, and in the flickering light of the wall torches the coffincar looked like a strange, enormous wheeled insect. The coffin itself was perched about a metre from the ground on a spindly metal undercarriage, connected to two sets of bath-chair wheels – large ones at the back and small ones at the front. Muesli's friend, Darceth, had made the chain-driven undercarriage in an old smithy he had discovered in the cellars of his castle. Darceth had also helped create the self-winding spring mechanism that powered the mobile resting-places. Another of Muesli's friends, Krazul, had designed the simple steering system of 'pull and push' iron rods that were attached to each side of the coffin. Over the years, the three friends had helped a number of vampires adapt their coffins in this way. Now, the sight of a vampire or two trundling round the night-dark lanes and alleys of Eyetooth in a coffincar was not at all unusual.

Muesli smiled to himself as he polished the black-enamel carrying handles. When he was finished he was going to put his coffincar back into his drive-in bedroom and go over to Countess Bray's to see if he could get her old runner going. He grinned as he worked with the polishing cloth. It was great to be back to normal again, with no more worries about having to leave Eyetooth. As his thoughts drifted pleasantly, a loud knocking on the outer gate startled him. Putting his polishing cloth down, he crossed the courtyard to the gate and opened it. His eyebrows lifted in surprise when he saw it was Count Fibula and about eight or nine other vampires. Two of the vampires held up torches and their flaring light threw distorted black shadows of the group on to the wall in the lane behind them. Count Corpus was there too, a strained expression on his face.

'What's up, Corpy?' Muesli asked lightly. 'Having a torchlight parade?'

The big policeman looked ashamed and shifted uncomfortably from one foot to the other. 'Mooz,' he said, then checked himself. 'I mean, Count Muesli ... no ... Moonsley ...' He stopped and glanced over his shoulder, frowning, at Count Fibula.

Count Fibula stared up at him angrily. 'Get on with it,' he snarled.

Corpus sighed heavily, turned back to Count Muesli and took a document from his inside pocket.

'It's my duty, Mooz,' he whispered, looking wretched. 'I have to do it. So sorry.' Then, speaking in a forced, official voice, he read from the document.

'"On evidence having been received from two independent witnesses that Count Moonsley, Vampire of Eyetooth, has been involved in a serious misdemeanour ... to wit ... the stealing of a decanter containing human blood belonging to Countess

Plaza, also of Eyetooth . . . it has become necessary to search the premises of the aforementioned Count Moonsley in order to ascertain the whereabouts of the aforementioned decanter.

'I hereby issue this Search Warrant.

'Signed. Count Fibula. Leader of the Council.'"

Corpus finished and looked miserably at his friend, who was standing with a shocked look on his face.

'I know this is all rubbish, Mooz,' he said. 'I had a real set-to with them in my office about it. But in the end there was nothing I could do. I have the signature of these two . . . witnesses . . . who say they saw you steal the decanter.' He curled his lip in disdain and looked coldly at the two vampires who were standing beside Count Fibula.

The shock that Count Muesli felt initially had faded slightly and was replaced by a strange bewilderment. He stared at the two accusing vampires. One was short, with pointed ears and thin lips, and the other tall, with staring eyes and twitching hands. They had their hoods back and returned his gaze with confident sneers on their pale features. Muesli recognized them. They were called Scabrus and Crusst and came from the other side of Eyetooth – a dark, maze-like area of the village where the nastier vampires lurked. Once or twice in the past Muesli had seen them at council meetings . . . and now he knew that he'd seen them much more recently too. These were the two hooded vampires from the Café in the Crypt. Count Muesli was confused. *Why were they doing this?*

'That's him,' hissed Scabrus, his lip curling disdainfully as he pointed at Muesli. 'That's the vampire who did it.'

Crusst sniffed and his features twisted in a sneer. 'He's no vampire,' he growled. 'He's a turncoat . . . a traitor to his blood heritage.' He spat at Muesli's feet. 'He's a *veggie*. That's why he stole the blood. He wants everyone to be like him.'

Count Muesli felt a hollow disappointment. Deep down he had always known that some vampires disliked him, but he had never thought that some would hate him *this much*. Steeling himself, he looked at Corpus and gave him a quick smile.

'It's all right, Corpy,' he said quietly. 'They can all come in and have a look around. I've got nothing to hide.' He pointed to Scabrus and Crusst. 'These two . . . gentlemen . . . are obviously mistaken. The sooner all this nonsense is settled, the better.'

Corpus nodded. 'That's what I think,' he replied, then he turned to Count Fibula with narrowed eyes. 'Carry on, Count,' he said. 'But I must tell you that I believe this is a waste of time . . . and wasting the police's time is an offence.'

Count Fibula's eyes narrowed. 'We'll soon find out, won't we?' he said softly and strode into the courtyard, followed by his servant, Ichor, and the other vampires. Accompanied by Scabrus and Crusst, he walked over to a wide door in the far corner and pointed. 'This is where we'll start,' he said and looked at Count Muesli, a barely controlled smirk on his face. 'What's in here?'

'My drive-in bedroom,' replied Count Muesli.

Fibula tried the handle. 'It's locked,' he said.

'I took my coffincar out for a spin earlier today,' said Count Muesli. 'I locked it after me.' He looked at Scabrus and Crusst meaningfully. 'You just never know who's hanging around these days.'

'Open it!' demanded Count Fibula.

Count Muesli took a key from his pocket. Unlocking the door, he pulled it open and stood back.

The other vampires pushed through the doorway and crowded into the room. Holding their torches high, they looked around them. On the walls of the vaulted room were dark hangings and old paintings in ornate frames. Enormous wrought-iron candlesticks stood in each corner, and against the walls were large, carved oak cupboards and bookcases overflowing with books and papers. As Fibula stood in the centre the other vampires moved around the room, searching in every nook and cranny. After a few moments they stopped, shaking their heads. They had found nothing.

'Well?' said Count Muesli grimly. 'Satisfied?'

A few of the vampires nodded and began to leave but a sneering Scabrus held up his hand. 'What's behind those curtains?' he asked, pointing to the heavy drapes that hung beside an ornate bookcase stuffed full of books. 'We seemed to have overlooked these.'

'Just a storage alcove,' replied Count Muesli.

'Let's see, shall we?' retorted Scabrus and pulled the curtain aside.

Muesli and Corpus gasped in unison.

There, on a shelf directly in front of them, stood a crystal decanter containing a few centilitres of dark-red blood. Around its neck hung a silver plaque engraved with the letter 'P'.

In the silence that followed, Count Muesli turned to Corpus. 'It's a set-up, Corpy,' he said clearly so that everyone would hear. 'Someone else stole that decanter, picked my locks and hid it in there.'

'Of course, Mooz!' cried Corpus, glaring angrily at Count Fibula. 'That's exactly what happened!'

One or two of the vampires nodded in agreement, but most of them, associates of Count Fibula, shook their heads, hissed and glared venomously at Count Muesli.

'Don't try and wriggle your way out of it, Muesli,' snapped Fibula, a triumphant look on his face. 'You've been caught in the act. Stealing the life-blood of another vampire is a particularly nasty crime.' His lips twisted and re-formed in a sneer. 'I have all the evidence I need. A trial is not required.' He turned and addressed the vampires, flinging out a pointing hand dramatically and exclaiming in a loud, harsh voice, 'Count "Muesli" is to be banished from Eyetooth!'

'What?' exclaimed Corpus in astonishment. 'But you must have a trial! It's the vampire law!'

Count Fibula sneered and curled his lip at Corpus. 'You obviously haven't read the small print,' he said. 'The leader of the council has the power *in exceptional circumstances* to make this kind of decision. *I* am the leader of the council at the moment, am I not?' he asked, turning to Ichor, Scabrus and Crusst.

All three nodded vigorously. 'You are,' they chorused.

'And I would say that these are *exceptional circumstances*, would you not agree?'

'We would,' they chorused again.

Count Fibula stared at Count Muesli, his eyes glittering in triumph. 'You are hereby banished from Eyetooth for a period of *twenty years* and are forbidden to have any contact with anyone from this place for that period.'

Count Muesli couldn't believe what he was hearing. *Twenty years?* He stood, numb and silent, as Fibula continued.

'Your house will be locked and shuttered and your possessions confiscated. If you do not leave now of your own accord, you will be removed from Eyetooth *by force.*'

There was an immediate outburst of mocking laughter from Ichor, Scabrus, Crusst and their cronies, but one or two of the others kept silent.

Fibula glared at Muesli with triumphant contempt. 'You will leave,' he hissed. 'Now!' Flicking a reptilian glance in Corpus's direction, he snarled sarcastically, 'As you are the upholder of the law here, you will make sure that Muesli leaves Eyetooth and then report back to me.'

Count Muesli sensed Corpus trembling with rage beside him and put his hand on his friend's arm to calm him down. He realized that there was absolutely no point in arguing with Fibula. He would have to accept the sentence for now and hope that he could prove his innocence and be able to return eventually. Outwardly he was calm but inwardly his thoughts were in turmoil. Taking a deep breath, he stared into Fibula's malevolent eyes, before turning and walking out of the gate into the lane. He was followed by the dejected figure of Corpus, his big shoulders drooping and his big, dark head shaking slowly from side to side in disbelief.

Chapter Nine

All the following day, Vinny went around with a fixed smile on his face which didn't fool anyone. They all knew that the filming wasn't going well. Nobody from the village had turned up to audition for the part of the vampire, Joe had run out of paint for the scenery and the sound equipment wasn't working properly.

'It's too old, Uncle Vinny,' said Samantha, as she and Joe tried to mend a connection in the recorder. 'You should get some new stuff.'

Vinny's false smile faded and he shrugged. 'Wish I could, Samantha, but the film's budget is already stretched as tightly as cling film over yesterday's roast. We'll just have to soldier on, I'm afraid. Make do and mend.'

Samantha sighed. 'We've mended this a few times already, but we'll do our best again.'

'Maybe I could change the script; take out the part of the nasty vampire?' suggested Nerys. 'That would solve one of the problems.'

Vinny shook his head. 'It's too good a part,' he said. 'Don't worry, we'll find someone to do it. I've got a feeling that something will turn up. Things will get better, you'll see.'

Joe looked at his father and saw him smile encouragingly.

'You'll see,' repeated Vinny.

It was an unusually quiet meal that evening. Nerys spent the entire time studying the script, Bill concentrated on eating, Granny Roz told Joe and Samantha a family story they had heard a hundred times before, and Vinny tried to crack a couple of limp jokes. After supper, as his mum and dad, Bill and Granny Roz played their usual game of cards in the caravan and Samantha wrote up her diary in her tent, Joe went for a walk around the tree-lined edge of the field. It was almost dark by now and the air was very still, as if the dusk was holding its breath. A few stars glimmered between patches of wispy cloud and, as it was a clear night, Joe glanced at the mountain, wondering if he would see the pointed crags of the summit. As usual, though, it was covered in mist, and Joe turned away and continued his walk.

As he finished his circuit and got back to the gate, he stopped and blinked. Someone was standing there; a slim, dark figure, bending slightly to peer at the notice Vinny had put up. A little prickle of fright tingled at the back of Joe's neck. He stepped back then stopped. Don't be such a scaredycat, he told himself fiercely. The whole family are only a few metres away, so you're perfectly safe. Anyway . . . who do you think it is . . . a vampire? Smiling to himself, he relaxed and walked forward again, peering at the figure. For a moment Joe thought it might be Dave, the farmer's teenage son, and was about to call out when the figure straightened up. Joe gasped and smiled at once. It *was* a vampire –

or, rather, someone wearing a vampire costume. The person was young and had a shock of orange hair. He wore an old-fashioned, high-buttoned black jacket, white shirt and floppy black bow-tie. A long black cape fell from his shoulders to the ground. It was obvious who he was and why he was here, thought Joe. He waved a hand in greeting.

'Hi!' he called cheerily. 'Have you come to audition for the part?'

The figure jerked round, stared at Joe in surprise and took a quick step backwards into the shadows of a big tree.

'Sorry if I gave you a fright,' Joe said, walking forward and opening the gate. 'I thought you had seen me.' He grinned and pointed at the caravan. 'Dad ... I mean *the director*, is in there. Come on, I'll tell him you're here. He'll be pleased somebody showed up.'

The figure took another step backwards.

Stage fright, thought Joe.

'Er ... would you prefer that the director came out to see you?' he asked.

'The ... director?' asked the stranger. It was a pleasant, light voice.

'Yeah,' Joe went on. 'Of the film.'

'Film?'

'*Vampires on Holiday.*'

'You're making a film?'

'Of course.'

Joe was beginning to wonder if the visitor had all his marbles.

There was a long pause before the visitor spoke again.

'I see,' he said softly and pointed to the gate. 'A film. Hence the notice.'

'Er, yeah,' replied Joe. 'Hence the notice.' He waited and, as there was no reply, he carried on. 'So, are you staying to audition or what?'

'I don't think I'd measure up,' the stranger said quietly, sadly. 'I'm afraid I'm a failure as a vampire.' He sighed and shook his head. 'I'll bid you goodnight.' He bowed and turned away.

'Hold on!' cried Joe. 'You can't go. We need another actor. I mean . . . why did you say you're a failure as a vampire? What happened? Were you in a play about vampires that didn't do well? You got a bad review . . . is that it?'

The stranger stopped and Joe thought he heard a sigh.

'Is that it?' Joe repeated.

'Something like that,' the visitor replied eventually, his back still to Joe.

'Well then,' retorted Joe, 'you should try again. You really should. Doing badly on stage is no big deal. Honest. It's like learning to ride a bike. If you fall off, you should get right back on again and have another go.' Joe winced. He was sounding just like his father, but he ploughed on encouragingly. 'Who knows . . . this time you might be a great vampire.'

There was another pause and then the stranger said, 'You think I might?'

'Of course!' cried Joe. 'Why don't you give it a try?' He pointed towards the caravan again. 'I'll get my dad. All right?'

The stranger turned and looked at Joe for a moment. Then he nodded and stepped out of the shadows.

'Why not,' he responded.

Joe saw now that the young man was good-looking and had a friendly, oval face. Maybe a bit on the young side, mused Joe, and not at all frightening to look at . . . but then he thought . . . Beggars can't be choosers and make-up can work wonders.

'Great,' enthused Joe. He turned and hurried towards the caravan. Halfway there, he stopped and looked back over his shoulder.

'My name's Joe. What's yours?'

The stranger smiled.

'My friends call me Muesli.'

Chapter Ten

Corpus sat at his desk and stared morosely at the wall. His best friend was gone and he felt awful. He had pleaded with Muesli to allow him to go with him into exile but Muesli had refused, saying it was better if he stayed put. That way, Muesli reasoned, there was always a chance that Corpus could prove his innocence. The big vampire groaned and tugged nervously at his thick, curly hair. How could he do that? He wasn't smart. The only reason he had wanted to be the policeman of Eyetooth was because he liked the look of the uniform. He fingered the jet buttons on the front of his black tunic, rubbed the back of his sleeve over the shiny badge pinned on his shoulder and groaned again. Vanity. That was all it was, vanity. He shook his head and took a deep breath. Come on now, Corpy, he said to himself, that's no way to think. Being sorry for yourself won't help Muesli.

The door burst open and Countess Alchema swept in. Her face was stern.

'I've just heard the news!' she cried angrily. 'Muesli kicked out of Eyetooth on some trumped-up charge. How could you let it happen?' She marched over to the desk and pointed a bone-white finger at Corpus accusingly. 'I thought you were supposed to be his friend?'

Corpus blinked shamefacedly. 'I tried to stop it, Countess, I really did,' he protested. 'But the accusations were made and appeared to be proved before I could draw breath. I was waving goodbye to Mooz before I realized what was happening.'

'Muesli was framed, of course,' stated Countess Alchema firmly.

'Of course he was!' Corpus shook his head, his shoulders slumping. 'Of course he was.'

The countess's eyes narrowed angrily.

'What we have to do is extract a confession from Scabrus and Crusst that they lied on oath.'

'But how are we going to do that?' cried Corpus. 'They'll never admit to lying.'

'Fibula,' said Countess Alchema darkly. 'He's behind this.' She folded her arms and stared at the large candle sconce by the side of the desk. 'He wants to bring back the dark ages,' she murmured, a strange light dancing in her eyes. 'And I freely admit it's a tempting idea. But the cost would be too high.' She shook her head firmly. 'We would be hunted down as before. In the end not even Eyetooth would be safe. So, Fibula must be stopped. Especially as his methods are so odious and underhand. Vampires are not without a sense of honour. They do not lie or cheat, but Fibula, to his shame, does both. He also encourages others to lie and cheat, which is worse. To get Scabrus and Crusst to lie, he must have offered them something in return.'

'Such as . . .?' Corpus wondered.

'As leader of the high council he could probably get them some money,' replied the countess, sitting down on the chair opposite him. 'But would that be enough to make Scabrus and Crusst lie on oath?' She shook her head thoughtfully. 'I don't think so. Perhaps Fibula promised them something else. Power, for instance?'

'Power?' said Corpus, surprised. 'The leader isn't able to dish out any power. He has to have every decision he takes agreed by the the high council.'

'But what if Fibula toppled the council and declared himself supreme leader? He could do what he wanted then, couldn't he?'

Corpus was startled. He hadn't thought Fibula's ambitions would go as far as that. He was shaken.

'He wouldn't dare . . . would he?'

Countess Alchema was about to reply when the door opened and in came Vane, Corpus's assistant. The little werewolf shook out his still-dry, ragged umbrella, carefully furled it and looked across the candlelit office at Alchema and Corpus. He nodded politely to the countess, then fixed his yellow eyes on his boss.

'Got a message for you,' he said brightly. 'From the council chamber. From Count Fibula himself.'

Corpus and Alchema shared a quick

74

glance, their eyes narrowed suspiciously.

'What does he want?' demanded Corpus.

'Wants you to go to his castle at once. Says you've to drop everything. And go,' added the werewolf redundantly.

Corpus stood up slowly. 'Thanks, Vane.' He looked down at the countess. 'Into the lion's den,' he said softly. 'I wonder what's on his mind?'

Chapter Eleven

'Ah!' cried Vinny delightedly as he hurried out of the caravan, closely followed by Nerys, Bill and Granny Roz. 'We have an audition at last!' He held out his hand to Count Muesli. 'I'm pleased to meet you Mister . . . er . . . Muesli.' He grinned. 'Nice name, but a bit, shall we say . . . *veggie* . . . for an actor playing a vampire? We'll have to change it to something a bit *beefier* if you get the part, won't we, ha ha!'

Muesli shrugged. 'We'll see,' he said politely.

'Of course we will,' replied Vinny. 'We've got plenty of time to think of one. We plan to be here until the end of next week.' He looked admiringly at Count Muesli's cloak. 'And, may I say, what a wonderful costume! So nice of you to go to all the trouble of getting dressed up. Now,' he rubbed his hands together briskly, 'shall we get started?' He pointed to the coffin, which was perched on the roof rack of the estate car. 'Let's do it beside that. More atmospheric!'

'By all means,' said Count Muesli as they walked past the campfire towards the coffin. 'What would you like me to do?'

'Right,' said Vinny, his eyes gleaming. 'The part you're auditioning for is Count Gristle, the nasty vampire in the story. Now, at the moment you look a bit too . . . shall we say . . . *nice* . . . to be taken seriously as a nasty vampire, but just give it your best shot, OK? Just imagine you are the nastiest, scariest vampire in the world and your aim is to frighten all of us out of our wits. Do you think you can do that?'

Count Muesli smiled. He was beginning to enjoy himself.

'I'll try,' he said. 'If you're really sure?'

Vinny nodded and smiled. 'That's it. Just do your best.'

Joe's instinct was to excuse himself and go to his tent. He didn't fancy the idea of being scared, even by an actor. But he told himself not to be such a wimp. Remember the dream, he thought. Be brave.

He and the others gathered round Vinny in a little group and gazed expectantly at the 'actor'. Muesli walked back a few paces and gazed at the coffin. He then turned to face them again and bowed his head. He began to chant under his breath ... strange, unintelligible words that seemed to wash over them like a warm wave, making them feel sleepy. For a few moments he just stood still, then, grasping the edges of his cloak, he pulled it over his head, at the same time dropping slowly into a crouch. Again he remained immobile for a few moments as the watchers gazed at him, mesmerized. Then he started to straighten up slowly. Still holding his cloak over his face, he stretched up ... and up ... like a black-draped column rising from the ground. And as his audience watched, they began to experience a vague feeling of unease. The black figure was still rising until (and nobody could remember this part of the performance afterwards) he left the ground and floated there, *his feet clearly centimetres above the grass*. The unease had now become the first stirrings of fear as everyone gaped, transfixed by the floating figure. Muesli suddenly screamed and threw back his arms, and his cloak spread out like the wings of a giant bat. The watchers jumped in fright. He came drifting towards them, arms still outstretched, fixing each in turn with his chilling stare, fangs bared, his scream dying to a hiss.

No one could move. Joe felt as if his feet had taken root . . . He couldn't even turn his head to look at the others, but he knew they were feeling exactly like him. Then suddenly it was over. Muesli closed his eyes, folded his arms across his chest, bowed his head and slowly descended to earth again. The shattered air seemed to breathe a sigh of relief, and all at once the spell was broken.

Joe and the others jerked and gasped as if waking from a nightmare.

'Was that all right?' Muesli asked mildly. 'Is that what you wanted?'

'Whoa . . .' said Vinny after a moment, gulping air and blinking. 'Yes . . . that was . . .' He trailed off and looked at the others for confirmation. 'That was . . . *something* . . . wasn't it?'

Joe nodded, his heart still racing. 'It was,' he replied slowly, taking a long, shuddering breath, '*really* something.' In a strange way, Joe felt elated. He had experienced something very scary and hadn't been reduced to a lump of quivering jelly as he thought he might. He had survived it.

Count Muesli bowed. 'Thank you,' he said.

'Right,' Vinny went on, gradually regaining his composure. 'Right then, Mister Muesli. I think I can safely say that you've got the part.'

'Absolutely,' Bill agreed fervently.

'Ah,' was all Count Muesli said. He suddenly realized he didn't know what he wanted to do in the future. This contact with humans had happened so abruptly and he had agreed to their request without thinking much about it. His 'act' had been easy. All vampires know how to mesmerize humans either by a look or by a way of speaking. How effective it was depended on how well the vampire used this ability – and how much the humans it was directed against were capable of being affected. Vampire-hunters, for instance, were reputed to be immune to it. Muesli had mesmerized his audience here to the extent that they remembered being frightened but not the fact that he had left the ground. For a few minutes while he was 'acting' he had been able to forget what had happened in Eyetooth ... but now it all came flooding back, the hurt, the loneliness, the worry. He had spent the entire day in a cave near the foot of the mountain, feeling desperately sorry for himself, and he had accepted Joe's friendly invitation because it made him feel better – it had hidden the bitter taste of being excluded.

His last image of Eyetooth was of his old friend Corpus, standing silently by the open gate, gazing forlornly after him. Muesli would miss his friends. He would miss his home and his life among others of his kind. But he had no choice. He would have to accept it. To have gone against the decision of the leader would have meant banishment forever. Corpus would try to prove his innocence. But would he be able to? Scabrus and Crusst had lied on oath and their word had been believed against his. He had been banished for twenty years, and that was that. In the life of a vampire it wasn't that long (it corresponded to about five years in the life of a human) but it meant loneliness, wandering, hiding. He heaved a long inward sigh. *So what should he do now?* The humans were certainly friendly and it would be fun to be a vampire acting the part of being a vampire . . . but then what? He frowned and looked around at the expectant faces. Best to consider it some more, he thought.

'Thank you. I'll think about it,' he said, bowing. 'But I must go now.' He turned and, without a backward glance, walked swiftly to the gate and out on to the lane, disappearing into the night.

Joe and the others looked after him in silence.

'Well,' said Nerys after a pause, 'that was quite a bit of acting, wasn't it? He was terrific at being scary.'

Joe looked at his dad. 'Do you really need to have something as scary as that in the movie, Dad? I mean, it's supposed to be a comedy.'

'Of course I do, Joe,' Vinny replied, a big grin on his face. 'It's contrast, you see. The funny bits will be funnier when they're contrasted with a bit of scariness.'

Bill nodded slowly. 'You're right, Vinny'

he said. 'The film would certainly be improved if Mister Muesli was in it. Let's hope he comes back.' He turned to Joe. 'Right, Joe?'

Joe gave a weak smile. 'Right,' he said, but he was not at all convinced.

Chapter Twelve

As pale clouds threw their veils across the moon, Count Fibula stood silently by the open window of his castle tower and gazed over the dark rooftops of Eyetooth. His eyes glittered with greed. Muesli was gone, and already Eyetooth felt better. Fibula gazed at the spires and towers of the other castles that pierced the gloom around him. All this will soon be mine, he gloated. The power I have here in Eyetooth as leader of the high council will be as nothing compared to the power I will have as dictator . . . as *emperor*! A thin smile twisted his lips. *Emperor*. Already he had decided not to continue with the 'testing'. It was too slow a procedure and was prone to mistakes. No . . . his next step would move things along faster. *Much* faster.

He turned, crossed the high chamber and hurried down the stone staircase to the great hall. He was expecting a visitor. A visitor who had a part to play in the next stage of his plan.

In the main hall Ichor was busy piling logs on the already-roaring fire. He jumped in fright at the sudden angry roar from the doorway.

'More logs?' yelled Fibula. 'Do you think I'm made of gold? Take them off at once!'

Ichor dutifully removed the logs he had put on the fire, laying them on the hearth and stamping on them to stop them smouldering. As he had his back to his master, he allowed himself a frown of regret. Fibula's castle was as cold as the grave and the great hall never got properly warmed up unless the fire was blazing like a furnace. But Fibula was mean and begrudged every log, so while the area immediately in front of the fire grew warm the rest of the room retained its icy chill.

Ichor turned to face Fibula, his expression

now one of apology. 'Sorry, Master,' he murmured ingratiatingly.

'So you should be,' snapped Fibula as he strode across the room and sat down on the great chair at the head of the table.

'The message was delivered, Count Fibula,' said Ichor after a moment. 'Your *guest* should be here shortly. The others are waiting in the ante-chamber.'

The baleful look on Fibula's face softened.

'Yes, excellent,' he snapped. 'Excellent.' He turned and gazed into the fire. 'Tomorrow evening I want you to fetch the . . . *servants* . . . the ones I pointed out to you earlier.'

Ichor blanched visibly. 'Fetch them, Master?' His voice was trembling. 'You mean . . . go down there and . . .' He gulped nervously. 'But no one's dared leave Eyetooth for half a century! Vampire-killers lurk everywhere, it's said.'

Fibula's eyes glittered angrily as he pointed a bony finger at his servant.

'You will have the honour of finding out if that's true, Ichor,' he snarled. 'You will do this or suffer the consequences. And believe me, those consequences will be far,

far worse for you than meeting a swift end at the hands of a vampire-killer.'

Ichor bowed his head. 'Y-yes, master,' he whispered.

'I am reasonably certain, however, that my proposed servants are not vampire-hunters but simple, ordinary humans,' Fibula went on. 'So . . . take the coach . . . It will impress them. Then, simply use *the voice* as you have been taught. There should be no trouble.'

'I will, Master,' replied Ichor obediently. 'I'll carry out your instructions.'

Just then, a banging on the great door made Fibula look up expectantly. He sat upright and placed his hands on the table in front of him, palms down, in a pose he felt was both commanding and regal. The anger left his face and a cold, hard stare took its place.

Corpus was ushered in a few moments later. The big vampire was obviously uneasy and unsure of what to expect.

Fibula noted this and crowed inwardly. He was beginning to instil fear already.

'Sit down, Count Corpus,' he said softly, gesturing towards a chair at the opposite end of the long table.

Corpus moved towards the chair but, instead of sitting down, he stood beside it, his hands behind his back. 'I prefer to stand,' he replied, then cleared his throat. 'What do you want?'

Fibula's eyes narrowed slightly. There was a note of defiance in the big vampire's tone. That won't last long, he thought. He looked down at his hands on the table top, then back to Corpus.

'You are the officer of the law in Eye-tooth, aren't you?'

Corpus was surprised by the question.

'Of course,' he retorted. 'You know that.'

'Yes, I do, don't I,' murmured Fibula, his eyes glittering. 'And I am leader of the high council, am I not?'

'Yes,' replied Corpus tersely.

Fibula smiled thinly. 'And you are an employee of the council, are you not?'

Corpus swallowed and cleared his throat again.

'I am,' he said slowly.

'Of course you are. And as such you not only answer directly *to* me but you take orders directly *from* me.'

Corpus stared at the venomous face before him.

'What orders?'

'In a moment,' replied Fibula. 'But first let me introduce you to your new colleagues.'

'Colleagues?' Corpus's eyes narrowed with suspicion. 'What colleagues?'

Fibula nodded to Ichor, who crossed to a door behind Corpus and opened it.

'The other policemen of Eyetooth,' Fibula murmured, the hint of a triumphant smile on his thin lips. 'Four, to be precise.'

Corpus stared blankly at Fibula. 'But I'm the only –' he began.

Fibula held up his hand. 'You *were* the only policeman in Eyetooth. I have appointed four more.'

Corpus heard footsteps behind him and turned to see four vampires approaching him from the adjoining room. Silver badges gleamed on the shoulders of all four. Two of the vampires Corpus recognized immediately as Scabrus and Crusst, but he didn't know the other two. One had a shaved head and was as big as himself, and the other was shorter but burly, with a thick mat of coarse hair and a drooping moustache. They walked past Corpus and, turning, stood by Fibula's chair, staring balefully back at the big vampire. At once Corpus saw that Scabrus and Crusst wore Chief of Police badges similar to his own. The other two vampires wore simple 'constable' badges.

Corpus looked at Fibula.

'You can't do this!' he cried. 'You require a meeting of the high council to appoint a policeman.'

'You haven't read the rulebook, Count,' Fibula sneered. 'A meeting of the *inner* council is all that is needed.'

Corpus clenched his jaws in frustration. Of course, he thought, the inner council . . . mostly Fibula's supporters. These new policemen were legal, after all.

'That wasn't the only thing that was decided,' Fibula went on smoothly, his eyes never leaving Corpus's face. 'I . . . *we* also decided that from now on a state of emergency exists in Eyetooth.'

Corpus was shocked. A state of emergency had never been declared before. It was supposed to be used as a last resort. It meant that the leader of the council had the power to arrest and imprison at will. It meant that Fibula could put as many of his opponents behind bars as he wanted.

'On what grounds was this decision made?' he asked stiffly.

'On the grounds that there are certain vampires in Eyetooth who are plotting to overthrow the high council,' replied Fibula.

'Rubbish!' retorted Corpus, his anger getting the better of him. 'That's nonsense, and you know it, Fibula!' His big shoulders quivered as he gripped the back of the chair tightly, trying to control his rage.

Count Fibula regarded the big vampire coldly. 'You could be one of them,' he murmured.

Corpus was so taken aback he could hardly think.

'What?' he blurted out at last. 'Are you accusing me of being a traitor to Eyetooth?'

'No,' retorted Fibula. 'Not as long as you follow orders. *My* orders.'

In a matter of a day or so, Corpus's whole world had turned upside down. Muesli had been exiled, and now he, Corpus, was being forced to obey the orders of a corrupt leader. If he refused he would be over-powered and thrown in prison. Once there, he would have no chance either to try and prove Muesli's innocence or to help his friends resist Fibula. He must stay out of prison as long as he could. But this meant doing Fibula's bidding. The very thought made him feel sick to his stomach, but it was the only way out.

At last he nodded slowly and took a deep breath. 'I understand,' he replied quietly.

'Just as well,' said Fibula. He sat back in his throne-like chair and regarded Corpus with a triumphant sneer. 'Now for your orders. You and your colleagues here will go at once and make your first arrest.'

'An arrest? Who are we to arrest?'

Fibula leaned forward, gripping the edge of the table with his talon-like fingers. He fixed Corpus with an icy stare.

'Countess Alchema.'

Chapter Thirteen

'I don't think that actor, what's his name
... Muesli ... is ever going to turn up,'
Vinny muttered, pacing up and down in
front of the caravan. 'We've waited all day.'
He glanced at his watch. 'Look at the time.
It'll be dark soon.'

'Never mind, Dad,' said Joe as he and
Samantha passed, carrying the sound equipment back to the car. 'We did get the family-
holiday scene filmed. And Granny Roz and
Mum were great as your vampire aunts.'

Vinny stopped pacing and smiled. 'Yes,
they were rather good, weren't they? They
took a bit of persuading, mind you, but it
was worth it in the end.'

'Never again,' said Joe's mum, shaking her head as she came out of the make-up tent. 'In future I stay strictly behind the camera.'

'Not me!' cried Granny Roz gleefully, emerging just behind her daughter-in-law. 'I love acting. I'm going to be a star!'

At that moment a clattering noise on the road made them all turn and stare. Round the corner swept a horse-drawn hearse, which drew up with a crunching of hooves on the small stones at the gate to the field.

It was a strange and magnificent sight. From the tips of the horses' ears to the elegantly curving springs that jutted out behind the tall back wheels, everything was black. Black as night. It was as if everything had been carved from jet and then magically given life. The hearse was imposing, with an intricately carved rail round the edge of the curved roof and tall, waving plumes at each corner. A row of arched and bevelled windows ran the length of the side, and the curtains that obscured them were swagged and tasselled. High up on the driver's seat sat a solitary coachman in a long trenchcoat and wide-brimmed hat. In one hand he held a long whip and in the other the reins for the pair of stamping, restless horses.

Everyone moved to the gate and stood, gazing in wonder.

Joe had seen a Victorian hearse once before, at a big transport museum, but this one was far more impressive. It must belong to a collector, he thought . . . or perhaps the local undertaker. He knew that some businesses used old vehicles as a gimmick to attract custom.

'Wow!' he said. 'That is something.'

'Fabulous,' breathed Samantha.

Vinny found his tongue.

'Fabulous?' he cried in delight. 'It's sensational! It's just what I need! Imagine if that thing was in the film! It would be . . .'

He stopped, beaming, lost for words for a moment, then called up to the coachman.

'Hello! What are you doing here?'

The coachman, a squat man with heavy eyebrows and glittering eyes, had been casting furtive glances around. He now looked down at them and nodded.

Joe noticed that he had irregular, strangely-shaped teeth.

'Good evening,' the coachman said in a

low, smooth voice. 'I have been asked to extend an invitation to you.'

The words seemed to hang in the air around them, echoey and compelling.

'An invitation?' said Bill, perplexed. 'From whom?'

'From my employer, Mr Fibula,' replied the coachman. 'He has a . . . *château* . . . not far from here. He has heard about your film and, as he is interested in moving pictures, he has extended an invitation to you to visit him. He says you may film in his house and you are welcome to stay as long as you like. He has accommodation for everyone.'

His voice sounded beautiful to everyone and they all looked at each other happily.

'A *château*,' said Samantha. 'That's like a castle, isn't it?'

'Exactly like a castle!' exclaimed Vinny, his eyes shining. 'What did I tell you?' he cried. 'Didn't I say something would turn up? Didn't I?'

Nerys nodded. 'So you did, dear. And I must say, it sounds wonderful.'

Vinny looked up at the coachman again. 'Could we use this hearse in our film?' he asked.

'My employer has told me to tell you that his entire household and effects are at your disposal.'

'Wonderful!' cried Vinny. It didn't occur to him or to any of them to ask why Mr Fibula had sent his messenger in an ancient, horse-drawn hearse. The coachman's voice had invaded the minds of all of them, making them feel that everything was as it should be.

'Mr Fibula must be absolutely movie mad,' Samantha whispered to Joe in delight. 'Imagine us staying in a *château*!'

'Yeah,' replied Joe slowly. 'Imagine.'

'When can we come?' asked Vinny excitedly.

'Don't be so forward, Vinny,' scolded Nerys.

'Not at all, madam,' replied the coach-man. 'My employer specifically requested that you should come now. This evening. He has everything prepared.'

'Everything prepared?' exclaimed Granny Roz. 'What are we waiting for? I don't know about the rest of you, but my old bones could do with a night or two in a proper bed. That bunk bed in the caravan is like concrete.'

'Right!' cried Vinny. 'That settles it. We're going now!' He turned to Joe. 'Quick, Joe,' he said. 'Fetch the camera. I want to get some shots of this magnificent contraption before the light goes. The rest of you . . . pack!'

As everyone bustled about, stuffing rucksacks and bags and striking the tents, Vinny filmed the hearse from every angle. He took shots of it standing in the road – long shots and close-ups – and filmed it as the coachman drove it into the neighbouring field then turned back into the lane. To finish, Vinny panned down from the top of the mountain to the hearse and horses waiting in the gathering darkness.

'Perfect!' he cried. 'This is going to look wonderful.'

'Are you ready?' asked the coachman, indicating the car, which was already full and had the caravan attached. 'We must go now.'

Vinny looked into the field and grinned. He had been filming for only half an hour or so, but everything had been organized. The rear of the car was full of luggage, bags were tied around the coffin on the roof rack and everyone was seated and ready to go.

'Wagons . . . roll!' he shouted, waving them on.

Nerys let out the clutch and slowly drove the car and caravan, bumping and swaying, out of the field and into the lane behind the hearse.

'Lead on!' cried Vinny, full of high spirits as he got into the car. 'Take us to your leader!'

At this the coachman gave a slight start.

'Leader?' he said with a nervous glance. Then, realizing that Vinny didn't mean it literally, he smiled faintly. 'Right,' he replied softly. 'Leader it is, sir.' With a shake of the reins, a crack of the whip and a muttered command, the coachman urged the horses into a trot.

Nerys changed up into third gear as they followed the hearse. 'He's going a bit fast, isn't he?' she said.

'Imagine,' said Granny Roz from the back seat. 'I'm going to sleep in a castle!'

Beside her Bill grinned. 'This film of yours is getting some good luck at last, Vinny,' he said, chortling. 'We might even get someone to play the villain, now that Mister Muesli hasn't turned up.'

'One of Mister Fibula's servants, maybe,'

replied Vinny with a broad grin. 'Who knows? Perhaps the butler!'

'Shouldn't we have left a note for the farmer, back at the field?' asked Samantha. 'To tell him why we're leaving?'

'I forgot about him,' said Vinny cheerily. 'But never mind. We're paid up until the end of the week, so it doesn't matter.'

Up ahead, the hearse suddenly veered to the left and bumped on to an overgrown track which led into the forest.

'He's going off the road,' commented Nerys and she slowed down so that the caravan wouldn't pitch over as she made the turn and followed the hearse.

Everyone had the same feeling that, although this was unusual, there was nothing to worry about. The coachman's soothing voice still echoed in their heads, calming and reassuring.

The track was narrow and, as the forest trees crowded in thickly on both sides, Nerys had to switch on her dipped head-lights. They illuminated the grass verge and the rear of the black coach as it trundled on ahead of them. For the first time she noticed that there was a large, scrolled 'F' etched into the glass of the curtained rear window.

'I must say this road isn't exactly what you would call a driveway, is it?' commented Granny Roz. 'My old bones are getting rattled to bits. Let's hope Mister Fibula's *château* is in better condition than this.'

Vinny turned round and winked cheerfully. 'Don't worry, Mum,' he said. 'He's probably an eccentric millionaire who couldn't care less about his driveway.'

They rattled along like this for few minutes more, until all of a sudden the hearse veered off the road again, this time to the right.

'Here we go again,' said Nerys as she followed it cautiously, easing the car and caravan through a narrow gap in the trees. 'Can hardly see a thing in here.'

The hearse was now forging a path through a thicket of fine branches which closed behind it then whipped across the windscreen of the car as it too went through.

As they bumped and rocked over tussocks and broken branches, Bill shook his head. 'This is a bit much!' he said mildly, peering out of his side-window. 'Where's the road?' The memory of the coachman's reassuring voice was beginning to fade somewhat.

'You tell me,' replied Nerys, staring ahead, trying to keep the coach in sight. 'Wherever this *château* is, it's well hidden.'

'Wow!' breathed Samantha. 'A *secret château*!'

Joe frowned. He had a vague feeling of unease. 'Do you think this is a good idea, Mum . . . Dad?' he said. 'Maybe we should turn back?'

'Can't turn round at the moment, Joe,' replied his mum. 'I'd have to wait for an open space.'

Just then the trees vanished and they found themselves following the hearse into a tunnel. The jolting journey suddenly became smoother as the car ran on to a made-up path, and everyone relaxed.

'This is more like it,' remarked Nerys. 'It feels like a proper road.'

'We must be going through the mountain,' said Joe, looking out at the rough-hewn walls, illuminated by the car's headlights. Then, after a few moments he added, 'Feels like we're going upwards.'

'Yes,' mused his mum. 'We are. I can only suppose that the *château* is on the other side of the mountain. We'll level out soon, I expect.'

'Doesn't look like it, Mum. The road's getting steeper,' said Joe.

'Mmm,' murmured his mum. 'This is unusual.'

'Oh, don't be such a miseryguts!' scoffed Vinny. 'It's an adventure. Live a little, why don't you! Perhaps our Mister Fibula lives at the top of the mountain – who knows?'

Joe felt a sudden lurch in the pit of his stomach. There was something he had been told about the top of the mountain . . . but what was it? He couldn't remember. His mind seemed to be filled with fog. He groped around in his memory for a few moments but eventually gave up.

All he was left with was an uncomfortable feeling that something wasn't right . . . and that they really shouldn't be doing this.

Chapter Fourteen

Count Muesli stirred, then opened his eyes. He was in complete darkness and, for a moment, he forgot where he was. The closeness of the walls was comforting, as was the padded lid just above his head – but it wasn't his own coffin, the one he slept in every day. Suddenly it all came back to him. After leaving the humans last night, he had wandered through the countryside, wondering what to do. As dawn approached, he found that he had walked in an enormous circle and had arrived back at the campsite. Tired and confused, he had spotted the comfortable-looking coffin on the roof rack of the car. Without giving the matter any thought, he had climbed in, lay down, closed the lid and immediately fell asleep.

But now he realized something was wrong. The car was moving.

He frowned. His instincts told him it was evening again, so why were the humans travelling? Hadn't they said they were to stay in the field for another week at least?

Reaching up, he lifted the heavy lid a little and slid it to one side. Looking up through the narrow gap, he was puzzled. Above his head a rocky surface swept past, illuminated from below by a yellowish light. Just as it dawned on him that the rocky surface was the roof of a tunnel and the illumination was from the car headlights, the car drove out of the tunnel and into the open air. Muesli saw the night sky appear above him, with tall, dark trees on either side and a misty moon riding high above them. With the force of a thunderbolt it came to him. Eyetooth! They were on the mountain . . . heading towards Eyetooth! What had possessed them? Why were they doing this? Didn't they realize the danger they were in?

Pushing the coffin lid out of his way, Muesli sat up anxiously. The first thing he saw was the back of the black hearse as it rumbled along in front of the car, the letter 'F' gleaming brightly in the headlights.

'Fibula!' he gasped in surprise. 'That's Fibula's hearse!'

He stared at it for a long moment, thinking hard. He should flee now, while there was still time. If he was found in Eyetooth, he would be banished forever. He had heard tales of other vampires who had been exiled for life – vampires who, once away from Eyetooth, had either been hunted down by the vampire-killers or had shrivelled away after only a few years. He did not desire either fate for himself. But nor did he want any harm to come to the humans from Fibula's dastardly hand. The leader of the council had obviously lured these unsuspecting people here for some dark purpose. Muesli was certain the car would follow the hearse straight to Fibula's castle and, once there, the humans would be trapped. It was against the ancient vampire code to harm guests, but Muesli was sure that would not stop Fibula. He tried to think clearly.

What should he do?

Gradually he realized the answer was obvious. He would have to risk capture and warn the humans. He couldn't stand by and allow Fibula to hurt innocent people.

Looking past the coach, he could see the turrets and towers of Eyetooth approaching through the darkness. He would have to act now, he thought grimly – the coach would be sweeping through the gates in a matter of minutes.

Gripping the edges of the coffin, he levered himself up until he was in a crouching position facing the coach. He could see the back of the coachman's head and shoulders. He'd know that hunched, squat figure anywhere. *Ichor!* Keeping his eyes on him in case Fibula's servant turned round, he manoeuvred himself on to one knee and prepared to climb out of the coffin. As he did so, his elbow caught the edge of the coffin lid. With a gasp of dismay he swung round and saw it slide off the edge of the roof rack. He knew that if it hit the road the sound would alert the coachman. Lunging forward, he grabbed hold of the lid's bevelled edge with his left hand and clung on, stopping it from falling past the car's windows on to the road. Then, bracing himself against the swaying motion of the car, he grasped the lid with both hands and slowly hauled the heavy object back on to the coffin.

Eyetooth was now much nearer and he realized he had no time to make another mistake. Quickly he wedged the lid inside the coffin beside him and climbed out on to the roof rack. Holding tightly to the edge of the coffin, he knelt down and gently lowered his head and shoulders over the edge so that he could look through the car windows.

The first thing he saw was the back of Bill's head. After a second, Bill moved to one side and Count Muesli found himself looking directly into Joe's face.

Joe's eyes and mouth opened wide in shock. Count Muesli responded by quickly making a winding motion with his hand to indicate that Joe should open the window. But Joe merely sat staring in disbelief, too shocked to respond. As they drove under the arched gateway of Eyetooth and along a narrow, twisting road between high walls, Muesli tapped on the window frantically, and this time he got a reaction.

Joe shouted, 'Muesli!' and Bill, Vinny and Samantha twisted round in their seats and gaped in astonishment. Nerys glanced over her shoulder, gasped and nearly drove the car into a wall. Muesli was almost shaken from his perch as the car swerved wildly, but he managed to cling on as Nerys regained control.

'What's going on?' she shrieked. 'What's he doing there?'

'It's Mister Muesli!' cried Vinny in delight as he recognized the face at the window. 'He's come to be in the film after all! Stop the car!'

At that moment the hearse drove through a stone archway into a wide courtyard and the car followed. The hearse stopped and Nerys applied the brakes, coming to a halt just behind it. The horses whinnied, stamping their hooves on the flagstones and tossing their black heads as the steam from their bodies rose into the night air.

Muesli immediately leapt to the ground and wrenched the back door open. His face was tight with anxiety. 'Drive away!' he hissed frantically. 'Drive away! You can't stay here!'

Muesli's obvious alarm got through to Nerys and she quickly let the clutch out and stamped on the accelerator. The car lurched forward . . . and promptly stalled. She turned the key in the ignition . . . once . . . twice . . . but the engine refused to start.

'It's flooded,' she said, looking back through her open window at Muesli. 'We'll have to wait a few minutes.'

'What's the problem, Mister Muesli,' enquired Vinny amiably, getting out of the car and looking around admiringly. 'This place looks hunky-dory to me!'

'You don't understand!' cried Muesli hoarsely, glancing over his shoulder in time to see Ichor climbing down from the coach. 'Get out and run! Run for your lives. Come on!' He reached into the car and grabbed Bill's arm.

'Hey! What's going on?' cried Bill, pulling his arm away. 'What are you up to?'

Joe quickly clambered over Bill's knees and scrambled out of the car, to stand beside Muesli. Swiftly he took in his surroundings. They were in the courtyard of a gloomy castle, surrounded by a high wall, and the only exit was the archway they had just come through. With its pointed windows and three narrow black towers, the front of the castle seemed to lean forward and hang over them. Hideous gargoyles

110

with bulging eyes and bared fangs stared down from the jagged battlements. Broad steps led up to the castle's great oak door in the central tower, and beyond the enclosing wall the towers and spires of other castles jutted darkly into the night sky. Joe didn't need his imagination to tell him that this place was scary. He could *feel* it.

Joe gasped, his eyes wide with alarm. 'This is Eyetooth, isn't it?'

'It is,' replied Muesli urgently, 'and you are all in grave danger. You must flee now!'

The realization hit Joe like a smack in the face. 'You're a vampire,' he said hoarsely. 'A *real* vampire, aren't you?'

Muesli nodded. 'A vampire . . . but a friend.'

'Muesli!' The astonished shout echoed round the courtyard as Ichor, now descended from the hearse, spotted the banished vampire by the side of the car. He started up the steps. 'Master, Master!' he screeched. 'He's here! Muesli's here!'

'Quickly!' Muesli cried beseechingly to Nerys. 'Try the car again!'

Once more Nerys turned the key, but again the engine failed to start.

A door opened in the tower to the left,

throwing a greenish patch of light down the stone steps and on to the courtyard, and out came Scabrus and Crusst with wine goblets in their hands. They hesitated for a moment as they took in the scene before them.

Nerys was still trying to start the car.

'I can't . . .' she muttered, then gasped as Joe reached in and tugged at her arm.

'Let's go, Mum!' he yelled frantically. 'Dad! Everyone! Those are vampires!'

'Vampires?' cried Vinny, walking round the car towards Joe and Muesli. 'What are you talking about, Joe?'

Granny Roz, Bill and Samantha got out of the car too, looking around curiously.

'Get him!' The shrill, enraged shout made every head turn towards the great door.

Count Fibula stood on the threshold, his bristling, furious shape silhouetted by the torchlight from within. 'The others can't escape. It's Muesli I want! Get him! Get *him*!' The voice was full of venom.

Scabrus and Crusst were galvanized into action. Scabrus pointed at the archway. 'You . . . Ichor . . . close the gates!' he screamed. 'We'll deal with this!'

Ichor immediately rushed towards the

archway, his broad-brimmed hat flying off as he ran.

Scabrus and Crusst dashed their goblets to the ground and leapt down the steps.

'Come on, come on. All of you!' shouted Muesli, trying to pull a bemused Vinny towards the gate.

'Come on, Dad! Everyone! Please!' wailed Joe.

'What does that man mean, we can't escape?' muttered Vinny in confusion. 'Why does he want you, Mister Muesli . . .?' He pulled his arm from Muesli's grasp and turned towards the car, right into the path of the onrushing Crusst.

With a vicious swipe, Crusst knocked Vinny to the ground and hurled himself at Muesli.

'Vinny!' screamed Nerys. She threw open her door, which struck the leaping Crusst full in the chest. The heavy blow knocked Crusst to the ground and he lay there, groaning. Joe had to jump backwards to avoid being knocked over.

Nerys tumbled out of the car to see to Vinny as Granny Roz turned and bolted back towards the caravan.

Scabrus, who had been right behind

Crusst, swerved to avoid the door but was thrown off balance and failed in his attempt to grab Muesli. Muesli leapt nimbly to one side and, as the thrashing form of Scabrus flew past him, planted a foot squarely in his back and kicked hard. The kick sent Scabrus sprawling across the flagstones. His head struck the bottom step of the staircase, dazing him.

The door in the other tower opened now and two more vampires emerged, running towards the car.

Joe felt he was back in his bad dream of the night before. He stood rooted to the spot, uncertain and confused.

'Muesli!' screamed Fibula, dancing up and down in his rage and gesticulating to them. 'It's Muesli, you fools! Catch him!'

Muesli turned to the family and hesitated. He realized that he couldn't help them now. He would have to look out for himself and save trying to rescue them until later.

Joe took in Muesli's stricken expression and knew for certain now that what the young vampire had said was true. Muesli *was* their friend. He had risked capture to try to save the family and was now in great danger himself.

Joe found his voice. 'Run, Muesli!' he cried urgently. 'Run!'

Muesli nodded, ashen-faced, then swiftly turned and ran towards the wall.

The two vampires changed course and made for the running figure.

Granny Roz suddenly appeared from behind the caravan. Swinging a walking stick in a low, scything motion, she struck the leading vampire across his shins as hard as she could. With a howl of surprise and pain the vampire stumbled and fell, clutching at his legs.

'Hit my boy, would you!' yelled Granny Roz and immediately bolted back inside the caravan and locked the door.

The other vampire raced on and caught up with Muesli by the courtyard wall. Muesli spun round and the two of them grappled together, the big, shaven-headed vampire slowly forcing Muesli lower and lower.

'No!' yelled Joe desperately, his eyes wide with concern. Again he felt as if he was in his dream, but this time he remembered how brave he had been. Before he knew what he was doing, he was racing towards the two wrestling figures. Reaching them, he hurled himself bodily at the big vampire, throwing him against the wall. The vampire's head cracked against the masonry and he let out a gasp of pain. Sinking to one knee, he released his grip on Muesli. At once Muesli climbed, as lightly as a squirrel, straight up the wall and on to the top. Astride the parapet, he halted and looked down. The big vampire was beginning to struggle to his feet.

Muesli fixed Joe with an urgent stare and leaned over as low as he could, extending his hand.

'Jump!' he said.

Joe jumped.

Muesli caught Joe's wrist and hauled him on to the top of the wall beside him.

From his vantage point Joe stared, wide-eyed and anxious, across the courtyard to where his family stood gaping at the three vampires who were getting to their feet around them.

'Mum! Dad!' he shouted.

His mum seemed to be the only one who was aware of what was happening.

'Go, Joe!' she shouted fiercely. 'Run! Get help!'

'We'll come back for your parents,' Muesli

hissed at his side. 'But we must go now!'

At that moment the vampire below them leapt upwards like a cat. Muesli twisted to one side, at the same time kicking out at the vampire, knocking him back down to the ground. The vampire fell heavily and lay, gasping, momentarily stunned.

Muesli gripped Joe's arm. 'Come on!' he cried and leapt lightly down on the other side of the wall. He caught Joe as the boy jumped down after him. They were in a narrow alley that wound upwards between high, dark castle walls on either side.

As Joe began to follow Muesli along the alley, he heard Fibula screech out an order.

'Bring them inside! Quickly!'

Joe faltered. What was going to happen to his family? Anxiously he looked up at the parapet of the wall. Maybe he should have stayed.

'Joe!'

Joe jerked round and saw Muesli staring at him in agitation, gesticulating urgently.

'Come now!' the young vampire hissed. 'Hurry!'

Breaking into a stumbling run, Joe followed Muesli along the narrow lane and into the mouth of a dark, cold passage.

Chapter Fifteen

Joe had a hard time keeping up with Muesli. The vampire ran as effortlessly as a flitting shadow – along narrow lanes, up and down flights of steps, through dark passages and across misty courtyards – until at last he stopped in the deep recess of a doorway.

Joe caught him up and stood beside him in the blackness, panting. 'Where are we?' he managed to gasp out at last. 'Where are we going?'

'We're here,' replied his companion, his voice low. 'Back door of a friend's house.'

'Won't they look for you here?' asked Joe anxiously.

'Possibly,' murmured Muesli. 'But I have several friends, so they have a number of places to think about. Anyway, we won't be staying long.'

'What about my parents and the others, Muesli?' Joe said, his pale face tight with worry. 'The vampires will bite them, won't they . . .?'

Muesli shook his head. 'I don't think Fibula will do that until he has us, Joe,' he replied quietly. 'We're witnesses.'

'But . . .'

The young vampire placed his finger to his lips. 'Shhh,' he whispered. 'We're going in.'

Turning the large, ornate, iron handle, Muesli pushed the door gently. It opened silently and he and Joe slipped through and into a darkened room. On the other side of the room a flickering light showed through the crack of a slightly open door. This provided enough light for Joe to see that they seemed to be in a small storeroom crammed with furniture and boxes. Heavy curtains hung from the walls on either side of the open door, and Joe kept close behind his companion as they crept towards it.

Muesli curled his fingers round the edge

of the door and peered into the room beyond.

Just as he did so, a large figure suddenly emerged from behind the heavy drapes beside them and hurled itself at Muesli. One word was roared out: 'Spy!'

Both bodies fell on to a nearby table with a crash, then dropped heavily to the floor.

'Muesli!' Joe yelled anxiously, jumping out of the way as the grappling figures rolled under his feet.

Muesli's attacker suddenly reared up, pinning Muesli under him. 'Muesli?' he gasped. 'Where's Muesli?'

'Here I am, you thundering great dolt!' snapped Muesli. 'I've come back, Corpy.'

Corpus reached out and pulled open the door so that the candlelight illuminated the whole room.

His great shaggy head shook from side to side in wonder as he saw whose chest he was sitting on. 'It *is* you!' he gasped in disbelief. 'I don't believe it.'

'It's true,' replied Muesli with a grin. 'But do you think you could get off me? I'm getting flattened here. I feel as if I've been hit by an avalanche!'

The large vampire leapt up with muttered

apologies and helped his friend to his feet.

'It's great to see you, but you shouldn't be here, you know, Mooz,' he said worriedly. 'You really shouldn't.' He glanced suspiciously at Joe. 'And who's this?'

'This is Joe,' said Muesli. 'An outsider.'

The big vampire nodded, mumbled a 'hello' and shook Joe's hand awkwardly.

'He has a big problem, Corpy,' Muesli went on. '*We* have a big problem. Fibula enticed his family here.'

'But they'll be all right until we can rescue them, won't they, Muesli?' interrupted Joe anxiously. 'Won't they? You said . . .'

Muesli nodded. 'I believe so, Joe,' he said. 'It's strictly against the ancient vampire code to harm guests . . . it's something vampires are very serious about. So Fibula dare not break that code until he is sure he has eliminated all the witnesses – you and me.'

'How many has he captured?' asked Corpus.

'Five. Four adults and a girl. I was with them but managed to get away with Joe. The others have been imprisoned by Fibula. We have to help them escape.'

Corpus's eyes widened and a look of

amazement filled his big face. 'Escape? I hardly recognize you, Mooz,' he said, shaking his head.

Muesli nodded. 'I know. I hardly recognize myself.' He was silent for a moment then he said, 'By the way, Corpy, Fibula seemed to have gathered a few little helpers. There was . . .'

Corpus held up his hand, frowning. 'I know,' he said miserably. 'Scabrus and Crusst and their two friends . . . Spitz and Horba.' He sighed. 'Things have changed since you left, Mooz. Changed fast. Fibula is making his move for power. Those four vampires? He's made them all policemen.'

Muesli gasped in disbelief. 'What? But . . . he can't do that! What about you? What about the council?'

Corpus shook his head. 'No one's stood up to him so far. He told me, if I refused to do as I was told, he'd have me dropped into a dungeon. And what good could I do there?' His shoulders slumped. 'It's a bad business, Mooz. He plans to round up what he calls "traitors to Eyetooth and plotters against the council" and throw them in jail. He's got one already.'

'Who?' demanded Muesli.

The big policeman sighed miserably. 'Countess Alchema.'

Muesli took in a sharp breath and clenched his fists. 'I should have known!' He stared at Corpus. 'They forced you to arrest her?'

Corpus nodded slowly. 'I couldn't bear to look her in the eye, Mooz. I felt like a slimy traitor. But I kept telling myself, do this now Corpus . . . stay out of jail and somehow . . . some way . . . you'll be able to stop this and turn the tables on Fibula.'

'You were right to do that,' Muesli said quietly. He took a deep breath. 'I'm glad I'm here. I've been too selfish. All I thought about was myself . . . and how miserable I felt. But when I woke up on the way here . . .'

Corpus blinked in puzzlement. 'Woke up?'

Muesli grinned. 'It's a long story, Corpy. Tell you later. When I woke up,' he continued, 'I saw that Joe here and his family were in grave danger from Fibula. I realized that the leader's plans were darker than I had imagined. I took a decision to help them . . . and although I'm a wanted man now, I don't regret it. Suddenly I feel as if I'm doing something worthwhile.'

'Countess Alchema says Fibula wants to be a dictator, Mooz,' said Corpus. 'Wants to have absolute power over all vampires. She says he must be stopped.'

'So that's it,' murmured Muesli grimly.

'If I still had the key, I'd let her out of jail and help her hide,' said Corpus morosely. 'But Fibula gave it to Spitz.'

'Muesli,' said Joe suddenly. 'Where will my family be? I'm so worried about them.'

Joe felt strangely calm. Here he was, living out the worst fears of his imagination: he and his family trapped . . . surrounded by vampires . . . and he wasn't panicking. It was almost like a hurdle race, he thought, with a number of barriers stretching out in front of him. What he had to do was concentrate on getting over each one safely.

'Fibula doesn't have dungeons in his castle, Joe,' replied Muesli, 'so they'll be locked in one of the rooms.'

'I suppose that's not so bad,' said Joe slowly. 'I just hate the idea of Mum and Dad and the others in some horrible, dripping, rat-infested place.'

Corpus shook his head. 'If it's rats you're

worried about . . . don't be,' he said. 'For some reason there are none in his castle. He has to buy them in.'

'Buy them in?' said Joe, frowning. 'What for?'

'Why, to drink . . .' Corpus faltered as he realized he was talking to a non-vampire. 'To . . . er . . . keep for . . .' He looked to Muesli for help, but Joe just nodded.

'Oh, I see,' he said and glanced from Corpus to Muesli, grimacing. 'For the blood, I suppose?'

'It's what vampires drink now,' replied Corpus almost apologetically. 'Up here in Eyetooth most of us have developed a taste for rat's blood. We can survive on it very well, you know. Human blood is not strictly necessary for a vampire's survival after the first few decades. It's just a habit that a lot of us find hard to shake . . .' He trailed off again, cleared his throat, then carried on brightly. 'But we don't all bite and drink blood. Oh no. My friend Muesli here hasn't touched a drop for years. He's strictly veggie.'

Joe stared at Muesli in surprise. 'Is that true?'

Muesli grinned and nodded his head.

'True. My real name is Moonsley but everyone calls me Muesli because I don't do the blood thing any more.'

Joe shook his head, smiling in amazement. 'A veggie vampire,' he murmured. 'Cool!'

'I presume that's an expression of approval?' asked Muesli.

Joe nodded and grinned. 'It means I think it's good.'

Muesli smiled. 'Thank you,' he said. 'But it's not what everyone thinks.'

'No,' said Corpus. 'Your enemies believe that you will lose your vampire powers and turn into a human, Mooz.'

'I'm not losing my powers, Corpy,' replied Muesli firmly. 'But I feel as if I can now *understand* humans. That's a good thing.' He clenched his fists. 'Our fight against Fibula starts now,' he said determinedly. 'And our first task is to free Joe's family . . . and tell as many of our friends as we can what Fibula is up to. Fibula still has a lot of support to gain before he can come right out in the open about his plans. At the moment he has to proceed with caution. He's manipulating the laws of Eyetooth for his own purposes, but there'll come a time when he won't even bother to use the law.'

'We'll have to keep you both out of his clutches,' said Corpus. He thought for a moment. 'I know just the place where you'll be safe. Remember that secret room that Countess Alchema showed us in her attic? They've searched her place, so they probably won't go back. Even if they do, they don't know about that room.'

Muesli shook his head. 'We can't afford to spend any time hiding, Corpy. We have to rescue Joe's family tonight.'

'Tonight?' said Corpus worriedly. 'Don't you think that's a bit too risky, Mooz? Fibula's men will be out looking for you by now.'

'Means they won't be expecting it, Corpy,' replied Muesli with a wink.

The big policeman's face slowly broke into a grin. 'You might be right,' he said. A sudden, furtive scrabbling sound from the hallway beyond the next room made him stop and put a finger to his lips.

'They're here already,' he hissed. 'Trying to get in at the front door. Could be any one of them.' He gestured towards the door to the lane. 'Come on,' he whispered. 'Time for us to go.'

Without a sound the three of them crossed the room and slipped through the door. Corpus took a key from his waistcoat pocket and locked it after them. 'Just as well I forgot to lock it earlier,' he muttered to himself.

Keeping to the blackest shadows, the three figures hurried along the lane and ducked into a narrow tunnel that led into the heart of Eyetooth.

It seemed that at least one of Fibula's searchers had been given the slip, but Muesli knew that he and his two companions could run into others at any moment. They had to trust to luck and their own stealth not to be captured before they reached Fibula's castle. Here's hoping our luck holds, he thought fervently. Here's hoping . . .

Trying to keep as close to the two vampires as possible, Joe was hoping too – hoping that their rescue mission would be successful, hoping that Muesli was right about Fibula not harming his family, and hoping against hope that they would all soon escape from this strange and frightening place.

Chapter Sixteen

'The outsiders are locked in the west tower, Master,' said Ichor, coming into the great hall where Count Fibula was standing by the fireplace. 'The old woman came out of the caravan as meekly as a lamb when we threatened to harm the others. She's a battling one. Nearly broke Horba's leg with that stick.'

'She'll pay,' growled Fibula. 'I'll save the dirtiest tasks for her when they're my servants. But I want no harm to come to them yet. Not until I have the boy . . . and Muesli is silenced. Then there will be no one to dispute my story that they came up here of their own free will. I have to move carefully, however. There are still too many of my enemies out there.' He stared into the fire, his eyes glittering at the thought of all that human blood so close ... so close. 'I've waited half a century,' he murmured to himself. 'I can wait a little longer.'

'We're sure to catch them soon, Master,' muttered Ichor. 'The four policemen are out searching.'

'I do believe Muesli has done me a great service,' mused Count Fibula as he paced up and down in front of his great fireplace. 'He has given me the opportunity to charge him not only with breaking the law in coming back to Eyetooth but also with consorting with outsiders to overthrow the elected council. He'll be given a life sentence of solitary confinement!'

'First we must catch him, Master,' ventured Ichor mildly.

Fibula rounded on his servant, eyes blazing.

'You have an unfortunate knack of stating the obvious, Ichor! Now let *me*. If you don't succeed in organizing the capture of Muesli and the boy before daylight, then you too will languish in prison.'

'I'll go out and join the search at once,'

the servant said meekly, bowing low as hc left the room.

A reverberating *doom* echoed through the castle as Ichor closed the great door. Fibula turned and walked towards a low archway in the corner of the room that led into the west tower. Once through, he began to climb the narrow, spiral stone staircase.

'A little look at my captives,' he muttered to himself as he moved slowly upwards. 'A little speculation as to which tasks they will perform . . . and another little look at those plump necks.'

Halfway up the tower was a small landing across which two iron-studded doors faced each other. Fibula carefully stepped up to the one on the right, which was secured by a large padlock. Keeping to the side of the door, he knelt down and, grasping an iron ring set in a narrow alcove, he gave it a twist to the right. A faint grating sound told him that the large and ancient booby-trapped flagstone just in front of the door was now secure and safe to stand on. Standing up again, he moved in front of the door and silently pulled aside the cover of a spyhole and peered into the small room.

The five occupants were all huddled together on a stone bench which stood against the opposite wall, unaware that they were being watched . . . and eavesdropped upon.

'It's not your fault, Uncle Vinny,' said Samantha. 'We all wanted to go. Didn't we?' she asked, looking round at the others, who nodded their heads miserably. 'We all felt as if we had to . . . like we were puppets or something.'

'Well, it's nice of you to say so, Samantha,' replied Vinny with a sigh. He got up and stared out through the high, narrow window at the night sky. 'But I blame myself. If I hadn't had that obsession with my vampire film, we wouldn't be in this mess.' He turned and leant against the wall despondently. 'When we get out of here, I'm going to chuck it straight into the bin.'

'And ruin my chances of being a star?' cried Granny Roz, sitting bolt upright and glaring at her son. 'You certainly will not, Vinny, my lad!'

'I wish I was out there with Joe,' Samantha said, kicking the end of the stone bench in frustration. 'Doing something to help you all. I feel so useless sitting here.'

'I know, Samantha,' said Nerys gently. 'I know. I hope Joe's all right,' she went on fervently. 'I hope he and Mister Muesli do manage to get help.'

'Me too, Nerys,' muttered Bill. 'Me too. He's a strange one, that Mister Muesli. I suppose he has to be a . . . you know . . . a vampire too. But he seemed to be on our side.'

'He *is* on our side, Bill,' retorted Nerys. 'Oh . . . I hope Joe is safe! I wonder what he's doing just now? I can't imagine my little boy running around a vampire-infested town. It's all so . . . so . . .'

She covered her face with her hands and Vinny put his arms round her.

'Don't worry, dear,' he said softly. 'I'm sure Joe will be fine with Mister Muesli. Did you see the way he tackled that big vampire? Our boy has turned out to be quite the plucky one, hasn't he?'

Nerys took a deep breath and straightened up. She smiled as she wiped her eyes. 'He certainly has, Vinny,' she said quietly. 'He certainly has.' She took another deep breath. 'Yes . . . Joe will be fine with Mister Muesli. He's a vampire but he obviously means to help. I'm sure he'll be able to get us out of here.'

Count Fibula quietly closed the spyhole and smirked. Poor fools, he thought as he activated the booby-trapped flagstone once more. Poor deluded fools. Going back down the stairs, he mulled over what he would do with each of his captives. Once Muesli and the boy were captured, his plan was to have the prisoners brought out one by one . . . down to the great hall for the initiation ceremony. He would lull them into a waking sleep with his *voice*, then . . . he licked his lips as he relished the thought . . . he would bite. One bite for each person . . . that's all it would take for them to be his slaves forever. Then he would have the servants that a vampire in his position needed.

Fibula reached the bottom of the stairs and went into his great hall, closing the tower door behind him. He crossed to the throne-like chair at the head of the long oaken table and sat down.

'Yes . . . servants at last,' he murmured with satisfaction, staring into the leaping flames in the grate. 'The old woman will tend the rats and the cesspit. The one they call Vinny will be my butler, the other man a footman. The woman and the boy and girl will clean and wash.' He looked around the great hall with its gargoyle-topped columns, iron chandeliers, velvet drapes and heavy furnishings thick with dust and cobwebs. 'This will be a palace fit for an emperor soon. Fibula . . . the Emperor of the Vampires.' His eyes glittered with greed and excitement.

He sat back and a slow smile spread across his grey features.

Not long now, he thought. Not long now.

Chapter Seventeen

Muesli, Corpus and Joe squeezed between two great outcrops of rock at the end of a narrow tunnel and emerged into a deep cloister at the corner of a small square. They were immediately aware of the *clop* of horses' hooves and the rumble of wheels. Moving quickly back into the blackness behind the cloister's pillars, they saw a tall, black, horse-drawn hearse drive by. Muesli caught a glimpse of a wizened white face and thin black figure reclining on black cushions. As the hearse disappeared from view, Corpus whispered, 'Count Zircon, Mooz. Off to the Café in the Crypt.'

Muesli chuckled, murmuring, 'Yes. Loves his ratburgers, does old Zircy.'

Moving out of the shadows carefully, they peered into the square. Tall castle buildings huddled together round this small paved area, crammed shoulder to shoulder as if jostling for space. One building, smaller than the others, had a squat, ugly look about it.

Corpus pointed to it and whispered to Joe, 'That's the jail. Fibula's castle is behind it. We get to it by going along that passageway.'

Joe looked where Corpus was pointing and saw the dark mouth of an arched entrance to the right of the jail.

'Who's guarding the prisoner, Corpy?' asked Muesli.

Corpus shook his head. 'Don't know,' he muttered. 'Maybe nobody. Scabrus and the others will be hunting for you. Although, come to think of it, Vane should be there. And if I know Vane, he'll be fast asleep.'

A lone coffincar emerged from a narrow passage not far away from them and trundled across the square.

Muesli smiled wistfully. 'Countess Bray,' he murmured. 'She managed to get it going after all.'

Joe gaped at the strange vehicle in

amazement. 'What is that?' he whispered.

Corpus bent down and whispered in Joe's ear. 'It's a coffincar, Joe,' he said, smiling. 'A mobile resting place. Invented by Muesli,' he added proudly. 'They're beginning to be quite popular.'

Joe grinned up at Muesli in admiration. 'It's cool!'

The vehicle disappeared from sight and they began to edge round the square. When they got to the opposite corner, they stood for a moment in the deep shadows of an arched doorway. Between them and the passage was an open space, dimly lit by a smouldering brazier. Muesli peered cautiously round the corner.

'Can't see anyone,' he murmured. 'Stay hidden. I'll go first.'

He moved out of the shadows, looked quickly to left and right, then hurried across the open space. He had taken only a few strides when the door of the jail opened and the large figure of Spitz emerged. The big, bald vampire paused in the doorway briefly to drop something in a pocket in his cloak. Caught in the open, Muesli froze. Spitz withdrew his hand from his pocket, pulled his cloak together and, turning, stepped into the square. He saw Muesli and immediately tensed, a slow, evil smile tightening his cheeks.

'Ah ... I've been looking for you,' he hissed, moving towards Muesli slowly. 'And here you are ... all alone, too. Aren't I the lucky one! I get the honour of capturing you.'

Before Muesli could react, Spitz was on him. For a big vampire he moved incredibly quickly, and Muesli staggered back under the force of his spring. He fell to the ground sideways, squirming violently to try and get away.

Spitz's strong fingers found his neck and Muesli gasped in pain as they tightened like a vice. He struggled to free himself from the murderous grip, but Spitz's fingers only seemd to to bite deeper into his flesh. No matter how much he twisted and fought, he couldn't get loose.

Suddenly the pressure was released and Muesli heard Spitz utter a muffled oath, his legs kicking out as he was dragged backwards. Muesli leapt to his feet, massaging the red weal on his neck, and saw Corpus with one arm round Spitz's throat and the other pulling Spitz's left hand up behind his back. Choking and trying to scratch at Corpus with his right hand, Spitz was hauled backwards towards the jail. As Joe appeared by Muesli's side, Corpus gasped out, 'Open the jail door, Mooz. We've got to get him inside!'

Muesli sprinted to the jail door and wrenched it open, and Coprus dragged the struggling Spitz through.

Joe and Muesli followed, closing the door behind them as Corpus expertly snapped handcuffs round the wrists of his heaving captive. Before Spitz had time to utter a word, Corpus pulled off his necktie and swiftly secured it across the bald vampire's snarling mouth. Then, feeling inside his cloak, he pulled out a length of strong cord, grabbed hold of Spitz's flailing feet and deftly tied them together. He stepped back a pace as the trussed vampire rolled over slowly and gazed up at the three of them with rage in his eyes.

Corpus leaned over him. 'You should've shouted, matey,' he said quietly, 'when you had the chance. Shouted loud enough to bring all your friends running. But you didn't, did you? Thought you'd get all the glory for yourself.'

He pulled Spitz's cloak aside, felt inside the lining and took out a key.

'The key to the cells,' he said triumphantly, showing it to Muesli and Joe.

'Well, old friend,' said Muesli with a wry smile. 'I'm very impressed. You tied Spitz up as neatly as a parcel. All we have to do now is post him off to the cells.'

'Don't often get a chance to show off my police skills,' said Corpus, beaming broadly.

Muesli frowned. 'But there's no going back now, Corpy. You're a wanted man, same as me.'

'About time, too,' replied Corpus with a grin. 'Now I won't have to take any more orders from Fibula. So let's do as much as we can before he finds out what's happened. I think we'll start by freeing the prisoner, don't you?'

Turning towards the door that led to the cells, they spotted Vane for the first time. He was crouched in a corner, eyes wide with apprehension, his rolled umbrella held in front of him like a sword.

Muesli realized at once that Vane could be in trouble with Fibula. He had done nothing to stop Spitz's capture and so might be regarded as their accomplice. Muesli didn't want to put the little werewolf in that dangerous position, so he stepped swiftly in front of Spitz's line of vision and winked at Vane.

'It's no use, Vane,' he said. 'Put down your weapon. You're outnumbered. I know you're just trying to do your job but it's hopeless. Surrender!'

Vane suddenly grasped what Muesli was doing. He jumped to his feet and brandished the umbrella, a grateful smile on his face.

'Come and get me!' he cried. 'You won't get Rufus Vane without a fight!'

Corpus rolled his eyes, grinned and leapt forward. He snatched the umbrella from the little werewolf, then they pretended to struggle with each other across the floor of the jail. After a moment, Corpus got Vane in a wrestling hold and dragged him towards the cells.

'Unhand me!' cried Vane. 'Let me go, you big oaf!'

Corpus pulled Vane through into the small hallway outside the cells area and closed the door behind them.

Letting the werewolf go, he grinned.

'Big oaf?' he said. 'Steady on there, Vane.'

Vane smiled sheepishly. 'Er . . . just acting along,' he said. 'Sorry about that. But thanks for making it look good in there. I'm not cut out for going on the run like you and Count Muesli.' He leaned close to Corpus. 'I hope things go well for you,' he whispered. 'Fibula is dangerous.'

Corpus nodded. 'He's taken some outsiders prisoner. The boy's family. We have to try to set them free. But,' he went on quietly, 'it's jail for you, Vane. Until tomorrow, probably.'

'Thanks, Count Corpus,' replied Vane. 'I won't forget this.' He leaned closer and pointed to the cells. 'Just so's you know,' he breathed. 'Grume's in there too. Spitz just brought him in. Fibula found out that the secret ingredient he was putting in Fangola was *carrot juice*. Accused him of being in league with Muesli. He's furious.'

Corpus was startled. 'Carrot juice? So that's what made it taste so good. No wonder Fibula's angry. He probably thinks Grume's been turning us all into veggies!' Shaking his head and grinning, Corpus opened the door to the cells and led Vane in.

The cells area consisted of a stone

corridor with four heavy, iron-studded doors on each side. Corpus unlocked the nearest one and Vane went in, closing it behind himself. As Corpus locked it again, Vane pointed through the tiny barred window to the door opposite and said quietly, 'Countess Alchema's in there ... Grume's down at the end. Good luck.'

The hall door was pushed open and Muesli and Joe came in, dragging a struggling Spitz by the rope round his ankles. The big vampire, mumbling curses behind the gag, was quickly pulled into an empty cell and locked in. Corpus promptly released Countess Alchema and Grume, and moments later everyone was standing in Corpus's office.

The countess and the owner of the Café in the Crypt listened intently as Muesli quickly explained what had happened and what they had decided to do.

'I'll go with you,' responded Alchema immediately and she turned to Grume. 'Is there somewhere nearby you can hide?' she asked. 'You won't be able to outrun anyone with that leg of yours.'

Grume nodded. 'Don't worry about me, Countess,' he replied. 'There are passages below the crypt that nobody but me knows about. I'll be all right there until all this fuss blows over.'

'Then go now,' insisted Muesli, 'quickly. And let's hope that the "fuss" blows over really soon.'

Chapter Eighteen

The night air breathed its chilliness around the stones of Eyetooth. Rooftops glistened dully and a thin mist drifted through the twisting, narrow lanes and alleys.

Muesli held up his hand and the others stopped. They were approaching the end of a damp and slimy stone passage. This opened on to the top of a staircase cut in the rock face opposite Fibula's castle. The staircase's worn steps descended steeply to the cobbled lane below and Muesli moved forward, peering cautiously downwards. Again he held up his hand, whispered, 'Someone's there,' over his shoulder, and turned to look out again. After a moment he relaxed. 'He's gone,' he murmured. 'It was probably one of Fibula's friends. He was in the lane, heading away from the castle.'

Countess Alchema, Corpus and Joe moved up to join Muesli, and they stood together, looking out on to the sheer, windowless back wall of Fibula's castle.

'So, you want to free the outsiders,' said the countess to Muesli softly, thoughtfully looking from him to Joe. 'Have you considered the consequences? What would stop them telling everyone in the outside world about us?'

'I can only ask them to give their word,' Muesli replied and looked at Joe. 'Would I get it, Joe? Would I get a promise from your family to keep our secret?'

Joe nodded firmly. 'I promise for them, Muesli,' he said. 'They won't say anything. Honestly.'

Count Muesli looked thoughtfully into Joe's eyes, then said decisively, 'I believe you.'

Countess Alchema shrugged. 'Then I'll have to believe it too.'

'So, Mooz . . .' Corpus muttered agitatedly, 'what's your plan? We're almost there. What do we do?'

'I've considered a few options, Corpy,' Muesli replied, 'but each one has its difficulties. We have to get inside that castle somehow, and in the end I think the simplest solution is best . . . climb the courtyard wall and break in through one of the windows. A straightforward frontal assult.'

Corpus beamed and cracked his knuckles. 'A frontal assault. I like the sound of that.'

'A trifle unsubtle, perhaps,' offered Countess Alchema. 'Why can't we use the boy here as a decoy? They don't know about your "treachery" yet, Corpus, so you could pretend to have captured him. That would bring Fibula out. Then we could rush in.'

Muesli shook his head. 'I thought of that, Countess,' he murmured. 'But it's very risky. Having Joe out in the open like that is asking for him to be captured. Supposing Fibula is suspicious and doesn't open the door? Supposing Scabrus and his cronies turn up? No, I think we should do it my way. We climb over the wall into the courtyard. Joe gets in the car and starts it on my signal . . .' He turned to Joe. 'Will the car start, Joe? And what about keys?'

Joe nodded. 'It should be all right now, Muesli . . . and there are spare keys in the glove compartment.'

'Good. So, Joe gets in the car and waits, you open the gates, Countess – they are only bolted on the inside – while Corpus and I break in through a window.'

Countess Alchema smiled. 'You've changed, Count Muesli,' she said. 'You're turning out to be a man of both leadership and action.'

'Let's hope this particular bit of action works,' responded Muesli, grinning back. He glanced down into the lane again. 'Come on,' he said softly. 'Nobody about. Let's go.'

Silently, the four of them hurried down the rock-cut steps. Turning right at the bottom, they ran to where the sheer wall stopped and the courtyard began.

'Over we go,' whispered Muesli.

Corpus knelt down beside Joe. 'On to my back, Joe,' he hissed. 'We're going straight up.'

Joe looked upwards and gasped. The wall was at least seven or eight metres high.

'How?' he whispered as he climbed on to

the policeman's broad back, gripping hold of the big shoulders firmly.

'Vampires are like squirrels when it comes to climbing, Joe,' Corpus hissed. 'No wall is a problem for us. Hang on tight.'

Corpus stood up and without a sound the three vampires leapt on to the wall, their strong fingers finding cracks and protrusions in the ancient stonework. Immediately, they began climbing, moving easily up the rough surface side by side, arms and legs bent and spread out like giant spiders. A moment later they reached the top and dropped down on the other side.

It was over so quickly that Joe hardly had time to register the thrill. It had been like riding on the back of a big, powerful animal. He slid to the ground with a grin on his face and they all crouched for a moment in the shadows by the wall as they got their bearings.

The clouds had obscured the moon again and a milky mist was beginning to drift down from the peaks and pointed roofs, merging with the mist at ground level.

Flames from a burning brand by the great door cast an orange glow over the steps and their dancing light flickered up the frontage of the castle.

'It would be nice if this mist became thicker,' said Muesli.

Joe pointed across the courtyard. The hearse was gone but the car and caravan still stood there. The torchlight gleamed fitfully on the brown paintwork of the caravan and the metallic blue of the car, casting long black shadows across the ancient paving.

'Start the car only when you see me come out with your family,' Muesli whispered.

Joe nodded and took a quick, shaky breath, tensing as he waited for the word.

'Very well . . . go!'

Joe stared across the gap for a second, then leapt to his feet. Keeping low, he raced across the courtyard towards the car. The others watched tensely as he reached it, opened the door and slid into the driver's seat.

'Get ready by the gates, Countess,' Muesli murmured. 'Don't open them until we come out.'

Countess Alchema nodded and, turning to Muesli and Corpus, touched each of them on the shoulder. 'Good luck!' she whispered and moved away around the wall.

Muesli and Corpus waited until they saw her slip out of sight behind one of the large stone pillars of the gate before beginning their approach to the castle. A series of thick buttresses supported the wall between them and the castle, and the two friends used these as cover, darting from one to the next until they reached the point where the wall joined the castle.

Muesli sprinted over to the door of the west tower and, listening for a moment to make sure no one was about to come out, he carefully turned the handle. He shook his head, mouthed the word 'locked', and he and Corpus immediately began to climb, crawling quickly and effortlessly straight up the rough-hewn surface, searching for a way in. Each window they came to was firmly bolted and the iron latticework was too strong for them to break through. Working their way across the castle front, they began to feel more and more frustrated. The castle was shut up tightly.

Eventually they split up, each taking one side of the castle, agreeing to meet again in five minutes.

Muesli moved up the left-hand side of the building, carefully investigating each window, but without any luck. Reaching the last locked window, he stood on the sill and held on to the carved lintel. Looking across the face of the building, he caught a glimpse of Corpus's big black shape crawling up the east tower. Beyond the east tower the shapes of other towers could be seen, black against the cloudy night sky. And around them towers and battlements, roofs and turrets – all merging together in the silent gloom. Turning to his left, he gazed at the giant stone needle of the west tower jutting into the darkness. Its windows seemed too narrow to allow entry – but, he thought, he could be wrong. Easing himself off the windowsill, he reached out, gripped the rough stonework and began moving, crab-wise, across the front of the castle towards the tower. A breath of wind made his cloak billow outwards and caused an eddy in the coils of thickening mist. Muesli gave a nod of satisfaction. The thicker the mist, the better.

The topmost window confirmed his fears. It was too narrow. Crawling quickly down the wall towards the next window

Muesli noticed a faint flicker of candlelight on the sill and stopped. The room was probably occupied, he thought, and he had no wish to risk being seen . . . but at the same time he wanted to know who was in there. Cautiously he eased himself lower until he was clinging to the wall to the right of the window which, he saw, was just as narrow as the one above. Throwing his head back as far he could, he leant to the left until he caught a glimpse of the inside of the room. He caught his breath and quickly pulled back out of sight. Joe's family were in there!

At that moment a touch on his shoulder made him twist round sharply.

'Corpus!' he whispered hoarsely.

'Found a way in!' the big vampire whispered back. 'Come on.'

Muesli tapped his friend on the arm and pointed to the window.

'The prisoners are in there.'

Corpus's eyes widened, then he grinned. 'Follow me,' he mouthed.

Climbing rapidly, they reached the parapet and slipped over it on to the gutter which ran along the base of the tiled roof.

'There's a skylight along here,' Corpus

whispered. 'It was locked, but the wood surround was rotten. I ripped up a big chunk and managed to pull the window open.'

Muesli's grin flashed white in the darkness. 'Well done, Corpy,' he whispered back. 'You're not called Corpuscles the Muscles for nothing!'

They began to move along the gutter when a sudden sound made them stop and look down into the mist-shrouded courtyard. A small door set into the large wooden gate opened and they were just able to make out the short, squat figure that climbed through.

The two friends quickly ducked behind the parapet wall and peered cautiously over the top.

'Ichor,' whispered Corpus, and Muesli nodded.

Fibula's servant agitatedly shook his head and rubbed his hands together as he hurried towards the castle. Muesli and Corpus held their breath as he neared the car, but Ichor scurried past without giving it a glance. Below them they heard the *doom* sound of the great door as Ichor entered the castle.

'Our little friend looks all of a twitter,'

murmured Muesli. 'I'll wager he's dis-covered that Countess Alchema and Grume have escaped and that his bald friend is in jail instead of them.'

Corpus nodded in agreement. 'He must've come back for the spare key. We don't have much time, Mooz.'

Muesli seemed deep in thought. 'Yes,' he replied after a moment, 'Ichor will release Spitz and the manhunt will be stepped up. Fibula will probably be able to persuade more of his friends to join them, now that there are four vampires on the run. We've given him the perfect excuse for claiming he's up against a conspiracy!' He frowned and shook his head. 'We've got to hurry. Come on!'

The two friends ran lightly along the gutter and across the glistening tiles until they reached the skylight that Corpus had opened.

Muesli looked around quickly. Eye-tooth's roofs and towers surrounded them, looming hazily through the mist, and he hoped that no sharp eyes were peering from their darkened windows. Hastily he slipped through the hatch after Corpus and found himself in an evil-smelling and dusty attic.

The moon shining through the watery clouds gave just enough light to make out heaps of shrouded furniture.

'There,' Muesli whispered and pointed to the dim outline of a door. Stepping carefully round the furniture and reaching the door, Muesli put his ear to it and listened. After a moment he gripped the iron ring handle, twisting it and pulling back slowly. The door opened soundlessly and the two friends peered out to see a narrow flight of wooden stairs leading down to a dark landing. Motioning Corpus through first, Muesli closed the door quietly behind them and they crept downwards.

By now their eyes were accustomed to the gloom and they could see that the wooden banister was broken and plaster was crumbling from the walls. Three peeling doors led off the landing . . . two were locked, but the third yielded to Muesli's tentative push and they saw that another stairway continued downwards on the other side. Heavy oak panelling lined the walls here, making the stairs seem even darker. A stone balustrade was in good repair but was thick with cobwebs and dust.

Creeping downwards through the silent

darkness, they reached another landing with three doors. Two of them led into empty rooms, but the third opened on to yet another staircase. As they went through this door and began to descend again, Muesli held up his hand and they stopped.

'Listen,' he whispered.

No far off they could hear the muffled sound of a voice raised in anger.

'It's Fibula,' Corpus whispered back after a moment, 'Ichor's told him about the jail.'

Muesli nodded. 'Sounds like they're in the great hall. This staircase should take us down somewhere behind it. We may be able to get to the west tower from there. Let's hope they don't decide to come out to check the prisoners, or we're in trouble.'

As they continued descending, the angry voice grew louder, but, just as they reached the bottom of the staircase, it stopped altogether. Muesli and Corpus stood, stock still, on the last step, straining to hear. After a moment, the *doom* of the front door closing echoed faintly through the castle.

'Ichor will have left with the other key,' Muesli whispered hoarsely. 'We must hurry.'

At the foot of the stairs loomed a

curtained alcove. Muesli gingerly pulled the drapes aside and peered through. A narrow hallway curved away into darkness on the other side. The large, iron-studded door to the great hall was on the left and further down the hall was a smaller door on the opposite wall. A wall sconce holding a guttering candle threw fitful yellow light. Gesturing for Corpus to follow, Muesli eased himself between the curtains. Treading as softly as they could and hardly daring to breathe, they passed the door to the great hall. A sudden faint scraping noise on the other side of the door made them freeze and they stood, stock still again, listening anxiously. Hearing no more noises, after a moment they tiptoed on and, reaching the smaller door, Muesli turned the handle quietly. The door swung inwards without a sound to reveal the foot of a spiral stone staircase. Muesli mouthed the words 'west tower' to Corpus and, nodding silently to each other, they passed through, closed the door gently behind them and began to climb.

Chapter Nineteen

Out in the courtyard, the chilly mist drifted like smoke around the car and caravan. Joe huddled low on the driver's seat, careful to keep his head below the level of the windows. He felt he had been waiting for hours but knew it could only have been fifteen minutes or so. There was a queasy, tense feeling in his stomach and he could feel a cold anxiety creeping inside him. Once or twice he had trembled and had to bite his lip to stop it. Someone had passed the car a little while ago and had gone into the castle. Joe had pressed himself further down into the worn leather of the seat, not daring to look out even after he heard the bang of the closing door.

I wish something would happen, he thought. I can't stand waiting like this much longer. I hope Muesli and Corpus are all right. I hope they find Mum, Dad and the others. I hope . . .

The sudden sound of the great door closing again made him jump. Instinctively he slid further down in his seat and lay there, eyes wide, hardly daring to breathe. After a moment he thought: perhaps it's Muesli with my family! Perhaps they're waiting for a signal from me! Levering himself up slightly, he craned his neck and peered hopefully over the dashboard. What he saw made him quickly hide again. Ichor had just come out of the castle and was now standing on the top step. Joe waited to hear the servant's footsteps go past, but there was no sound. The seconds ticked by, and still there were no footsteps. He's not moving, thought Joe. What's he doing?

Curiosity got the better of his anxiety and slowly Joe levered himself up and peered out again. He frowned as he squinted throught the hazy darkness. The torch on the wall was guttering now, on the point of going out, and it was difficult to see much. Ichor seemed to be struggling with something that had got stuck in his cloak. Joe stared harder and saw the torchlight glint off a metal object. It was a key, he realized – a large key which somehow Ichor had managed to get entangled in his clothing. As Joe watched, Ichor at last wrenched the offending object free and hurried down the steps.

Joe slid down quickly again and held his breath. Ichor's footsteps pattered towards the car and Joe's heart leapt. He's going to look inside the car, Joe thought, and he lay as still as he could, his heart pounding. He's bound to see me! The footsteps reached the front of the car, paused, then hurried on past. Joe closed his eyes and let out a long, slow breath of relief as he realized that Fibula's servant was making for the gate.

Easing his head up once more, Joe looked out. Ichor was indeed hurrying away from him towards the gate, but halfway across the courtyard he stopped as a dull, reverberating *thump* echoed from the castle. The noise startled Joe. Peering cautiously over the dashboard, he saw Ichor swivel round and stare up at the west tower. A moment later there was another *thump*, not so loud this time.

Something's happened up there, thought Joe anxiously, I wonder what? Ichor was now racing back towards the castle, cloak flying. As he reached the great door, Joe heard the grinding of a key as it was unlocked from the inside. The door was pulled hurriedly open and the agitated figure of Count Fibula stood there, silhouetted against the torchlight from within.

Joe didn't dare move. He kept still, hoping he would not be noticed.

'Did you hear it?' demanded Fibula eagerly, his voice harsh with excitement. 'The noise from the tower?'

'I did, Master,' gasped Ichor. 'It sounded like the trapdoor in the tower opening and then closing again.'

'That's exactly what it was!' Fibula almost dancing with excitement. 'The trapdoor!'

'Someone's fallen through,' said Ichor slowly. He looked up at the tower, then turned back to Fibula, puzzlement in his voice. 'But how did he get in?'

Fibula gave a short, triumphant laugh. 'That's not important. All that matters is that we've caught someone. So . . . let's go and see which of the escaped rats is in the trap!'

Joe heard Ichor's high-pitched, excited laugh recede as he followed Fibula into the castle. He lay back on his seat, stunned. Muesli! They had caught Muesli! He was sure of it. Some kind of trapdoor, they had said. Up in the tower. He sat up quickly, his heart racing. His family must be imprisoned there. And what about Corpus? Was he caught too? Joe's eyes roamed up the dark, mist-shrouded stonework of the west tower, searching for a clue to what had happened. After a moment, one of the lower windows was lit briefly as a torch was carried past. He tensed, his hands gripping the edge of the dashboard.

Ichor and Fibula were climbing the tower to investigate. Joe clenched his fists and shook his head in desperation. He must *do* something. What should he do? *What should he do?* Suddenly a faint but distinct screech of laughter came from the tower, followed by another . . . and another. The laughter continued for a few seconds, then it died away to silence. Joe strained but could hear nothing else. Cold anxiety flooded through him and chilled his whole body. Fibula and Ichor had been laughing in triumph and Joe knew in his heart that it was because both Muesli *and* Corpus had been captured.

Twisting round in his seat, he stared at the gateway, trying desperately to see Countess Alchema. The fading torchlight by the great door didn't reach that far, and both the pillars and the gateway were shrouded in darkness. Joe peered harder but couldn't tell if she was there or not. He turned back to look again at the great door. *What should he do?* Should he call out? No . . . that would focus attention on him – and what if there were other vampires around? It was too dangerous to shout for Alchema.

From the back of his mind there came the faint echo of a familiar word – 'scaredy-cat'. He screwed up his eyes and bunched his fists, shutting the word out by concentrating on the image of a closed door, a trick his dad had taught him. As he did so, he suddenly had a thought. A door . . . the great door of the castle . . . it was shut . . . *but maybe it wasn't locked*. He remembered Ichor slamming it behind himself and

Fibula as they rushed inside, but he was almost sure that in their excitement they had forgotten to lock it. It was madness, he knew, to even think about going into the castle, but what else could he do? Surely the unlocked door was a sign? An invitation for him to go and help? A swift glance over his shoulder told him that Countess Alchema was still not in sight. When he turned back, he had decided: he was going to do it.

Taking a deep breath, he opened the car door, jumped out and bounded up the steps to the great door. At that moment the torchlight flickered and died, leaving Joe in complete darkness. The night seemed to press in on him then, its cold, damp breath on his shoulders and neck. Anxiously he fumbled and felt his way along the studded surface of the oak door. Its timbers were weathered smooth with age and felt slippery and almost alive under his touch. Joe shuddered. He could easily imagine it as the carapace of a gigantic beetle. At last he found the iron ring that was the door handle. Gripping it with both hands, he took a deep breath, twisted it to the right and pushed. The door opened and, without stopping to think further, Joe slipped inside and closed the door behind him.

He stood for a second, trying to get his bearings, his eyes darting to left and right, his heart hammering loudly in his ears. The large, gloomy entrance hall he found himself in was poorly lit by a single candle in a wrought-iron candelabrum. Tall, narrow doors stood on either side of a stone staircase that stretched upwards into the shadows. Heavy, dark-red curtains hung beside all the doors, and even in the fitful, yellow light Joe could see they were encrusted with cobwebs and the dust and grime of centuries. It seemed colder here than it had been outside, and Joe shivered as he tried to decide what to do and where to go. The staircase must be the most logical place to start. To reach the tower room he would have to go upwards, so hopefully if he went up this staircase he would find a way into the tower.

Keeping close to the stone balustrade on the right-hand side, he crept stealthily upwards. After twenty steps he reached a landing and saw that the staircase branched to right and left. Hugging the balustrade like a lifeline, he followed it round to the right and began climbing again. The light from the candle below became fainter and darkness began to close in around him. A few more steps, and a noise from below made him stiffen, the hairs on his neck prickling with fright. Breathing as quietly as he could, he waited and listened, his heart beating wildly.

When, after a few moments, there were no more sounds and he was able to breathe more easily, he began to climb once more. Twenty more steps took him to another landing and, as his eyes adjusted to the dark, he was able to make out the shapes of doors facing him. This must be the first floor, he thought. *So, which way?* After a moment he realized it was obvious. He had turned back on himself coming up the stairs, so the west tower should be on his right. His hand still on the balustrade, he began to move across the gloomy landing towards the hallway on the other side.

A sudden, soft, rustling sound made him glance downwards and he froze in horror. The black shape of a vampire was rushing silently up the staircase towards him, hands reaching out and cloak flying. Shocked, Joe gasped and started backwards. All his senses were screaming at him to run, but he couldn't. He was transfixed. The figure reached the top of the staircase and came towards him. From below, the faint candle-light briefly shone on silver hair.

Joe's eyes widened. 'Countess Alchema?' he said hoarsely, hopefully, as the dark shape loomed over him.

'Yes, Joe!' hissed the countess, reaching out and gripping his arm. Joe almost fainted with relief. 'I saw what happened and followed you in! You're going the wrong way! We can't reach the tower from here. We have to go through the great hall . . . Come on!'

Still holding on to Joe's arm, she led the way back downstairs.

'I've been here before,' the countess whispered as they reached the bottom. 'A long time ago. This used to be Countess Bray's home before Fibula cheated her out of it with forged documents.' She pointed to one of the doors in the hallway. 'The great hall is through here.' Countess Alchema pushed the door open and, after cautiously peering round it, she turned back to Joe. 'They're still in the tower,' she hissed. 'Quickly . . . follow me!'

She darted through the door and Joe slipped after her, quietly closing the heavy oaken door behind him.

The great hall lay empty, the smouldering logs in the wide fireplace bursting into fitful flame, filling the room with undulating, deep black shadows. Just like a movie set, thought Joe as he took in the vaulted ceiling, the stone columns and gargoyles, the heavy velvet curtains and the throne-like chair by the long table. Dad would love to film in here. Joe's concern for his family, pushed away by the excitement of the last few minutes, now returned with a vengeance. He winced. *I hope they're all right! I hope . . . I hope . . .*

Keeping close to the tall shape of Countess Alchema, Joe crossed the great hall. As they headed for an arched doorway in the far corner of the room, the countess explained about the trapdoor.

They had almost reached the door-way when they heard noises on the other side. Countess Alchema seized him by the arm and pulled him roughly behind a curtain. Joe stood there tensely in the stifling, dusty darkness beside her motion-less figure, hardly daring to breathe as the door opened and Fibula and Ichor came in.

Fibula uttered a harsh laugh. 'It's all so easy,' he said. 'We'll soon find the boy and Alchema . . . and the one-legged shopkeeper can't have gone far.'

'No, Master,' Ichor replied gloatingly. 'I'll fetch Spitz from the jail now and tell the others. We'll soon find them.'

Joe and the countess heard their footsteps recede across the hall, and a moment later came the sound of the great door closing. Alchema tensed. Moving her hand up slowly, she gently pulled back the curtain and peered out. Joe looked too, carefully holding the edge of the heavy fabric close to his face and squinting round it.

He saw Fibula standing with his back to them, staring into the fire. Half turning, the vampire lifted his hand and threw a heavy object on to the great table, before turning back to the fire. The object hit the table with a hard, sharp sound, skidded a short distance, then came to a rest. It had hardly stopped moving before Countess Alchema had sprung from her hiding place, leapt across the room and snatched it up. Taken by surprise at the countess's sudden movement, Joe could only stand and stare, the curtain still clutched in front of him.

Fibula spun round, startled, and stared at Countess Alchema in surprise ... an expression instantly transformed into violent anger.

'You!' he spat out. His eyes darted to the key which Alchema held in her fist. 'Give me that.' His voice dropped suddenly to a much lower register and became persuasive, wheedling. 'You don't want it. What would you do with it? Give it back to me.'

The countess drew herself up haughtily. 'You dare to try the voice on me, Fibula? On me?'

Fibula's face contorted in a vicious snarl. 'You're right, of course,' he said. 'I'll just take it.' He took a step forward, and Alchema held up her hand.

'Stop!' she cried and, as Fibula hesitated, Countess Alchema turned quickly to Joe. 'Joe! Catch!'

She threw the key and Joe leapt from his hiding place and caught it.

Fibula saw Joe for the first time and his eyes widened in surprise.

'The boy!'

'Go! Free them!' cried Alchema.

'Stay!' commanded Fibula, his voice deep

again, deep and dreamlike. 'Do not move, boy.'

Joe stood by the doorway, swaying in indecision. Fibula's voice rang in his head and he found it hard to listen to anything else. He wanted to move but couldn't. Then suddenly his mind cleared and he was aware that Countess Alchema was singing, a high, sharp succession of strange, off-key notes that shattered the hypnotic effect of Fibula's voice.

Fibula was staring at Alchema, his grey face now a mask of cruelty and hate, red eyes glittering with fury and dark lips open, revealing yellow fangs. He spread out his arms, seeming to grow taller as he did so, and Joe realized with a horrified start that Fibula was floating . . . his feet were centimetres above the flagstones. Alchema's singing had now become an unearthly howl and Joe saw that *she was floating, too*.

He watched, awestruck, as the two vampires fixed each other with penetrating, baleful stares and began to drift slowly in a wide arc, circling like boxers in a ring. The air in the room seemed suddenly heavy, as if a tremendous storm was approaching, and Joe found it difficult to breathe.

He stared blankly at the circling vampires, a strange drowsiness slowly overtaking him, and he almost felt as if he was floating, too . . . as if he was hovering, weightless, in the thick air.

All at once Alchema's howl stopped and she turned her face quickly to Joe. Her eyes were bright and fierce and Joe felt their burning power. 'Go!' she cried, the word cracking through the air like a gunshot.

The sharp command jerked Joe out of his trance. Turning, he stumbled towards the door. As he pulled it open and ran through, Alchema let out a piercing scream and launched herself at Fibula.

Chapter Twenty

Count Muesli stared out of the narrow window and sighed.

'Rats in a trap, Corpy,' he said with bitterness. 'That's what Fibula called us and that's what we are. Brainless rats.' He turned and leaned against the wall, shaking his head.

'My fault,' replied Corpus regretfully. 'You asked me to hold back, but I was too eager. It was probably my weight that tripped the mechanism. And,' he added mournfully, 'my weight that broke your arm when we fell through into this prison.' He pointed to Muesli's right arm, which was now in a sling and bound with strips torn from Vinny's shirt. 'Does it still hurt?'

Muesli smiled ruefully. 'A bit,' he replied, 'but I'll survive. And if it makes you feel any better, I think the trapdoor would have been activated by the lightest of steps.'

Corpus shrugged glumly. After a moment he said, 'You'll figure some way of getting us all out, won't you, Mooz?'

'Don't see how,' Bill butted in glumly, flopping despondently on to the stone bench beside Granny Roz. 'We've been thinking about how to get out ever since we arrived, but with no luck.' He glanced up at Muesli and Corpus, suddenly hopeful. 'How about if you two turn into bats? Then you could fly out of here . . .'

Muesli shook his head and smiled wryly. 'That's a myth,' he said. 'Started by Hollywood. Vampires are not shape-shifters like werewolves.'

'Thought as much,' muttered Bill morosely, slumping forward with his head in his hands.

'Oh, come on, Bill,' Vinny said, smiling gamely and shivering as he pulled the lapels of his jacket together across the remnants of his shirt. 'Never say die.'

'Never say die?' Bill shot back. 'We're walking vampire dinners, the lot of us!'

'And what about Joe?' interjected Nerys anxiously. 'He's out there, hiding in the car. They're bound to find him! We've got to try and think of a way to save him!' She turned to the two vampires. 'Is there really any chance of escape, Mister Muesli? Really?'

Corpus shuffled his feet and Count Muesli frowned.

'It's possible that Corpus and I could fight our way out when they come for us,' he replied slowly. 'Then in the confusion you could make your escape.'

'A fight? With that broken arm of yours?' said Bill sceptically.

'Yes! A fight!' cried Granny Roz, jumping up agitatedly. 'Good. You know, I'm so angry with those bloodsuckers I could . . . I could really . . .' She shook her head grimly and balled up her fists. 'I could really punch one of them on the nose.'

Vinny grinned tiredly and patted his mother's arm. 'That's my little mum.'

'I would!' protested Granny Roz.

Muesli smiled. 'If it comes to a fight, madam,' he said kindly, 'the best thing you can do is run.' Suddenly his head went up and he stiffened, holding his good hand up for quiet.

Everyone listened and they heard a faint, high-pitched sound drifting up from somewhere in the castle.

'What is that?' Vinny asked 'That weird noise?'

Samantha caught the significant look that passed between Corpus and Muesli.

'You know . . . don't you,' she said to them quietly.

The sounds stopped and Muesli turned to her, nodding slowly. 'It's the noise a vampire makes when it attacks another vampire,' he replied hesitantly. 'It means that somewhere in this castle there are vampires fighting.'

A silence grew in the room now as everyone caught their breath and listened. After a few moments Muesli and Corpus glanced at each other again, frowns on their faces. Corpus turned to the family and put his finger to his lips, demanding quiet.

Muesli crept soundlessly up the stairs and, crouching, listened intently at the door. After a moment he half turned and addressed the upturned, expectant faces.

'Someone's running up the stairs,' he whispered, still listening. 'A light step . . .' He stopped and slowly stood upright. 'A very light step,' he murmured, then spoke loudly, startling everyone, 'Joe?! Stop where you are. Don't move!'

'Joe?' gasped Nerys. 'Mister Muesli, you . . .'

'Shh!' said Corpus hoarsely.

From the other side of the door came a tremulous voice.

'Mum? Dad?'

'Joe!' cried Vinny and Nerys together joyously. 'Joe!' Galvanized into action, they tried to run up the stairs to join Muesli at the door but were stopped by the big arm of Corpus.

'Wait!' he ordered.

'Joe, it's Muesli,' said Muesli, his mouth close to the door. 'Have you stopped moving?'

'I have. Muesli . . .?'

'Yes?'

'It's all right. I know about the trapdoor . . .'

Muesli nodded. 'Good.'

'. . . and I have the key!'

'That's wonderful!' cried Nerys.

'Oh, Joe, you're terrific!' exclaimed Vinny.

Muesli looked down at the family's tired

179

but shining faces and hushed them once more.

'Muesli,' Joe was saying, his voice urgent. 'We have to hurry . . .'

'I understand, Joe,' replied Muesli, turning back to the door. 'Now listen . . . look around you. There must be a handle or ring or control of some sort. You have to find it and make the trapdoor safe to stand on. Can you see anything like that?'

There was a short silence, then Joe said, 'Yes! There's a big iron ring in an alcove here. Could that be it?'

'Try it, Joe,' replied Muesli. 'Turn it.'

Muesli listened, his ear to the door, and heard Joe grunt.

'It's hard to turn?' he asked.

'V-very . . .' grunted Joe, his voice hoarse with effort. 'But it's . . . moving . . . it's moving . . . got it!'

Everyone heard a grating sound, like old rusty bolts sliding into place.

'Now try stepping with one foot on the large flagstone in front of the door, Joe,' said Muesli. 'Hold on to something as you do it!'

'It's all right,' Joe called after a moment. 'I stamped on it to make sure it was safe. It is!'

A moment later, the bolts were drawn, a key turned in the lock and the door swung open, revealing Joe standing agitatedly on the threshold.

The family rushed up the steps and gathered round him excitedly, everyone talking at once. But Joe was distracted and wouldn't stand still for the hugs and kisses.

'Muesli!' he called. 'Muesli!'

Everyone turned to the young vampire as he bent and stared into Joe's anxious face.

'It's . . .' Joe stared at Muesli's arm. 'What happened? You OK?'

'A small accident, Joe,' Muesli replied quickly. 'It's nothing. Now . . . what is it . . .?'

'Countess Alchema, Muesli . . .' Joe gasped out, wide-eyed. 'She's in the big hall . . . fighting with Fibula!'

Muesli straightened immediately and beckoned urgently to Corpus. 'Come on, Corpy,' he cried. 'The rest of you . . . keep together and follow . . . but not too close!'

The two vampires sped down the staircase, their feet barely touching the steps. Following more slowly, the family picked their way down in the feeble light of the small candle they had taken from their prison.

Seconds later, Muesli and Corpus burst into the great hall to find a scene of devastation. Curtains had been torn down, furniture smashed, candelabra overturned and smouldering logs lay scattered over the flagstones. At first glance there seemed to be no one in the room, but as they edged forward they heard a snuffling sound coming from behind the great table. Corpus ran round the table as Muesli, holding his injured arm close to his body, leapt lightly on to the top and then over the other side. There were two figures on the floor, locked in the final throes of a violent struggle. Fibula was kneeling beside the prone and feebly writhing figure of Alchema, his hands closed round her throat as she weakly tried to fend him off. Breathing heavily, Fibula pressed down harder and harder, staring into Alchema's desperate face as she gasped for breath. Muesli saw that their faces and hands were streaked with blood and their cloaks were ripped.

Fibula uttered a thin howl of anger as he was bodily wrenched off his victim by

Corpus, but he was too weak to resist. His last energy had been spent and he could do nothing as Corpus tore his cape from his shoulders, ripped it into ragged lengths and bound him hand and foot.

Muesli gently wiped the blood from Alchema's face with his cloak.

'Countess . . .' he said hoarsely, 'Countess . . . are you badly hurt?'

Countess Alchema's mouth twitched in an attempt at a smile. 'It's nothing,' she whispered weakly. 'A few scratches, that's all.'

Muesli glanced at the dark blood that glistened on the tears in her clothing and he grimaced. He knew the damage that vampire teeth and talons could do.

'You need rest and attention,' he insisted. 'Let's get you away from here.'

Corpus appeared by his side and, without a word, bent down and picked up Alchema as easily as if she weighed no more than a sack of feathers.

Joe came into the room, followed by his mum and dad, Bill, Samantha and Granny Roz. Seeing Fibula lying trussed and inert, he smiled in delight – but his face fell as Corpus appeared from the other side of the table with his burden.

'Countess!' Joe cried, running to her. 'Countess!'

'She'll be fine, Joe,' Muesli said reassuringly.

Joe's family gathered behind him and his mum put her hands on his shoulders.

'A friend, Joe?' she asked gently.

'Countess Alchema, Mum,' replied Joe. 'She fought Fibula so I could bring you the key. She's wonderful.'

The countess smiled and shook her head slowly.

'You're the wonderful one, Joe,' she murmured. 'I was unsure what to do, but you decided for me.'

The countess looked at Nerys. 'He went into the castle . . . I simply followed. He's a brave boy.'

'I know, Countess,' replied Nerys softly, squeezing Joe's shoulders. 'I know.'

'And now we must get out,' said Muesli firmly, 'before Ichor comes back with the others. Come on.' He turned and quickly led the way into the hall, watched with cold and impotent fury by the bound and gagged figure of Count Fibula, lying prone on the flagstones.

The dark courtyard was deserted as they

hurried from the castle, and the humped shapes of the car and caravan loomed through the mist as they approached. Above them the moonlight filtered through the cloud vapour, creating a faint, eerie glow.

As Corpus carried Alchema towards the gate, Nerys ran to the car and slid into the driver's seat. She looked up as the others approached.

'Fingers crossed,' she muttered and turned the key.

The big engine barked a few times then started, its first coughing roar dying to a steady, satisfying rumble.

'Yes!' cried Bill. 'We're out of here!'

'I'll ride in the caravan!' cried Granny Roz, running to the door and climbing in.

'What's Uncle Vinny doing?' said Samantha, puzzled, as she and Bill got into the car.

They looked round to see that Vinny had opened the tailgate and was hauling something out.

'You can't be serious!' cried Bill as he realized that Vinny now had the camera in his hands and was filming the castle, which was briefly illuminated by the watery moonlight.

'Too good an opportunity to miss,' cried Vinny gleefully, his old enthusiasm flooding back. 'Too good!' He climbed into the back seat beside Bill and kept filming as Nerys carefully eased the car and caravan in a long curve, heading for the gate.

Joe and Muesli trotted beside the car, Joe looking up anxiously into the preoccupied face of the young vampire.

'What are you going to do now?' he asked.

Muesli frowned. 'First thing . . . guide you and your family to freedom.' He glanced quickly at Joe. 'I'll have to accompany you. The mountain is riddled with tunnels . . . you could all get lost.'

'And Corpus . . . and Alchema . . .?'

'Corpus will take care of her,' Muesli said as they reached the gate.

Having set Countess Alchema down to sit on the edge of a horse trough, Corpus drew the big bolts and pulled the gates wide, peering cautiously into the lane.

'All clear,' he announced over his shoulder, waving the car on urgently. 'Go. Go!' Muesli turned to Corpus. 'I'll have to go with them,' he said quietly. 'To lead them out.'

Corpus looked at him in puzzlement. 'You mean, *we'll* have to go,' he replied.

Muesli shook his head. 'You have to stay and make sure that Countess Alchema is all right. You can hide with her in the secret room.'

'No, Mooz,' protested Corpus in a whisper. 'Can't do that. I'm too big to hide. Anyway, I don't want to miss the fun. I'll help the countess to get home, then I'll join you, all right?'

Before Muesli could reply, a rattling sound made them jerk round. Out of an alley about thirty metres away a coffincar appeared and turned towards them.

Corpus tensed, ready for action, but Muesli smiled.

'It's Countess Bray,' he said as the vehicle drew near.

'Muesli!' called the countess, bringing the coffincar to a halt beside them. 'Heard all about the shenanigans tonight.' She scratched her mane of wind-tangled hair with both hands and wiped some dirt from her eyes. 'Was stopped by those infernal swine Scabrus and Crusst not long ago on the other side of Eyetooth and they asked if I'd seen you. They're very cocky . . . very confident . . . told me about you being hunted.'

She glanced through the gateway at Joe, standing by the car full of curious faces, and then at Alchema, sitting on the pillar.

'Didn't tell me about all this, though!' She peered hard at Muesli. 'You've been in the wars, too, I see. This all about Fibula being dastardly, is it?'

Muesli nodded.

'Don't need to know anything else!' she boomed. 'How can I help?'

Muesli glanced at Corpus's suddenly hopeful face and then nodded at Countess Bray. 'Alchema's in a weak condition, Bray,' he answered. 'Could you take her home? She fought Fibula to a standstill.'

'Did she, now! Ha! Always knew she had grit! Bring her over – perch her behind me.'

'I certainly will!' cried Corpus in delight, then, leaning down, he whispered, 'I knew we'd be going together, Mooz.'

As Corpus helped Alchema walk to the coffincar, Countess Bray said, 'Scabrus and Crusst are too far away to worry about at the moment, Muesli. Any others in the equation?'

'Spitz is locked up in the jail and Ichor is

off to free him. So we probably have a few minutes' grace. There's another . . . Horba . . . but I don't know where he is. Could be close. We'll have to be quick.'

'I understand,' she replied briskly. 'Time is of the essence.'

Alchema was helped aboard and she leaned on Countess Bray's back, holding on to her waist as tightly as she was able.

'Don't worry,' she assured them tiredly as Joe, Muesli and Corpus said goodbye. 'I'll be fine in hiding. And it might be an idea for you two to do the same . . . far away from Eyetooth. Perhaps the humans will shelter you.'

Corpus raised his hand in farewell and Muesli bowed. 'Goodbye, Countess,' he said, 'and good luck.'

'I'll keep her out of Fibula's clutches . . . don't you worry,' said Countess Bray firmly. 'Now . . . off we go!' She released the brake and the coffincar rolled quietly away down the alley into the swirling mist. Picking up speed on the slope, it turned into a narrow passage and disappeared from sight.

Muesli turned to Corpus. 'Alchema's right, Corpus. We'll go. Fibula may assume that she's gone with us. If he does, then he won't search for her.'

'We'll come back, Mooz,' said Corpus defiantly. 'Once you're better.'

'Yes,' agreed Muesli ruefully. 'I'm not much good to anyone like this.'

Corpus gave his friend a sympathetic look, then walked back to the caravan and climbed in. Joe got into the back of the car beside Samantha, Bill and Vinny. Muesli eased himself into the front seat beside Nerys as Joe said, 'I heard what Countess Alchema said, Muesli . . . about us sheltering you and Corpus.' He leaned forward in his seat and gripped his mother's arm. 'That would be all right, wouldn't it, Mum? Muesli and Corpus could stay with us for a little while?'

Nerys looked at Muesli and nodded. 'We're in your debt,' she said quietly. 'You must stay with us until you are better. We'll look after you.'

'Absolutely!' added Vinny.

Muesli didn't respond for a moment, then he nodded slightly. 'Thank you,' he replied. 'You're very kind.' He pointed to the lane. 'And now we must go. Quickly. Turn left.'

Nerys took a deep breath, engaged first gear and drove the car and caravan carefully through the archway, turning left into the narrow, high-sided lane. The mist, which had been thinning, suddenly grew thicker and she switched on the headlights.

'No lights,' said Muesli quietly, and Nerys quickly switched them off again. 'Right here,' he said tersely as a dark opening loomed. Cautiously Nerys turned right into the mouth of a pitch-black tunnel: a hollowed-out cleft that ran through a massive spur of rock. Instinctively she reached for the light switch, but Muesli swiftly said, 'No.'

Peering ahead intently, he leaned over and steered the car with his left hand until they emerged from the tunnel a few seconds later.

They were now on a twisting, cobbled road, bounded on one side by sheer rock and on the other by high stone walls. The mist lifted slightly and just ahead Nerys saw another archway approaching. On either side of it she could see curving stone buttresses and above it dark battlements pierced by narrow slits.

Muesli pointed to the opening. 'Once through there,' he muttered, 'we will be out of Eyetooth.'

The tense silence that had filled the car evaporated and everyone let out sighs of relief.

'We've made it!' cried Bill.

'Home and dry!' whooped Vinny in delight.

Muesli didn't reply. He had been scanning the approaching archway worriedly and now he leant forward and stared into the deep shadows under the projecting battlements.

'What is it?' asked Joe anxiously.

'Thought I saw something up there,' murmured Muesli. 'Something moving.' He continued to stare upwards as the car swept under the archway and out on to the mountain track. 'Must've been mistak –'

'Muesli!' cried Joe, who was looking out of the back window. 'Something just landed on the caravan!'

The young vampire twisted round in his seat and groaned as he struck his injured arm against the dashboard. Fighting the pain, he peered past Bill and Vinny. 'Can't see anything,' he gasped.

'A big black shape lying on the roof!' exclaimed Joe.

'I can see it too!' cried Samantha.

Vinny squirmed round, stuck his camera out through the open window and pointed it at the caravan.

'Will I stop, Mister Muesli?' asked Nerys, a note of panic in her voice.

'No! Keep going,' urged Muesli. 'Whatever happens, you mustn't stop. I'll look out.' Rolling down his window he leaned out as far as he could. Around him the mist swept past in drifting gusts, the bright moon giving it a strange, silvery glow. The silver-white vapour turned the rocks and stunted bushes into ghostly shapes and drifted like cold breath over the track, which wound steeply downwards towards the mass of dark firs that covered most of the mountain. As he twisted round, Muesli saw a face staring down at him from the top of the caravan. It was a broad face with a thick tangle of black hair and a heavy moustache, and it glared at him with malevolence as its owner clung to the roof of the swaying vehicle. Muesli recognized him right away. This was the fourth member of Fibula's search team, the one whose whereabouts couldn't be accounted for.

'Horba!'

The thick-set vampire bared his teeth and reared up into a crouching position, ready to leap. Bright moonlight suddenly found a way through the clouds, flooding the car and caravan with a milky luminescence. At the same moment the door of the caravan swung open and Corpus appeared. He was behind Horba and the crouching vampire hadn't seen him. Corpus's eyes met Muesli's and he winked. Gripping the caravan's gutter rail with one hand and the top of the door with the other, Corpus tensed and, with one mighty, twisting, acrobatic vault, landed on the roof beside Horba.

Horba spun round in surprise and Corpus, ducking low, leapt forward and pushed him hard in the chest.

Muesli caught a glimpse of the surprised look on Horba's face as he toppled from the roof, arms and legs thrashing, cloak flapping. The burly vampire landed heavily among the stunted bushes by the side of the track, rolling over a few times before they saw him shakily rise to his knees and glare with fury at the receding caravan.

Granny Roz stuck her head out of the open caravan door and shook her fist at the groggy figure as it disappeared from sight around a turn in the track. 'Good riddance to bad rubbish!' she yelled gleefully, before popping back inside again.

Vinny brought his camera back into the car.

'What a shot!' he crowed.

Muesli looked up at his old friend, who was now sitting on the roof. 'Well done, Corpy,' he cried above the roar of the engine and the crunching noise of the tyres on the small stones that peppered the rough track.

Corpus nodded and grinned, his wild hair blowing about his face in the rushing wind. 'Must say I enjoyed that,' he shouted back. He threw a quick glance over his shoulder towards Eyetooth, lost in the thick mist, and shook his head. 'But I wonder when I'll drink my next glass of Fangola.' Rolling on to his side, the big vampire slipped lithely over the edge and swung himself through the caravan's open door. Before he closed it, he called out, 'How's the arm, Mooz?'

Muesli shrugged wryly. 'Could be better,

I suppose. Sorry it has come to this, Corpy. But we'll come back. Fibula will have me . . . and you . . . banished forever now . . . but we'll come back and win. Fibula hasn't heard the last of Mooz and Corpy!'

Corpus beamed. 'You're dead right!' he exclaimed, the slipstream snatching at his words and carrying them off into the hurrying mist. 'We're not finished with him. Not by a long chalk.'

He laughed and closed the door.

Sitting back in his seat once more, Muesli gazed pensively out at the dark pines as they swept by on either side of the car. He transferred his gaze to the track as it descended steeply in a tight curve, and after a moment he saw ahead the dark mouth of the long, twisting tunnel that would take his companions to safety and him and Corpus away from their home.

No one spoke. Nerys was concentrating on her driving, while Bill and Samantha lay back in their seats, looking out at the thin, streaming mist.

Vinny stared silently down at the movie camera that he held between his knees. Absent-mindedly he flipped the lens cap on and off . . . on and off.

Joe was lost in his thoughts. Tiredness washed over him and he felt his eyelids drooping. I'll sleep, he thought, and when I wake up perhaps I'll find that this has all been a dream. He smiled faintly as his eyes closed. No, he told himself drowsily, this was no dream. This happened . . . *to me*! A feeling of elation surged through his weariness and his smile widened as he thought of what he would do when he got home. He would go straight to that old tree with his friends and stick his hand . . . no . . . *both hands* . . . into the empty eye. No one would call him a scaredy-cat ever again.

Epilogue

Joe promised Muesli that his family would keep Eyetooth's secret – but will they? How hard will it be for them to have two vampires in their home without it becoming known?

How long will it be before Fibula is able to send his emissaries into the world to begin creating his vampire empire? And if the biting begins again, how long will it be before the vampire-hunters return?

As the car drives out of the tunnel, eases through the thicket at the foot of the mountain and swings on to the forest track, the secrecy of Eyetooth and the defeat of Fibula are on Muesli's mind.

The others, temporarily perhaps, seem to have forgotten about the evil schemer up on the dark mountain.

From the caravan comes the sound of wild singing – 'She'll be coming round the mountain' – warbled in a high soprano and rumbling bass as Granny Roz tries to teach the old car journey favourite to Corpus.

Joe is asleep, his head resting on his father's shoulder.

Vinny is back to his old, optimistic self, telling Bill, Nerys and Samantha exactly how he's going to finish his film. He's got big plans for it and is very excited. This time, he says, it's going to be a hit.

He may be right. People like to laugh at their fears, and a vampire comedy might be just the thing they need.

They should laugh while they can be-cause if Fibula gets his way . . . *they might not be laughing about vampires for very long.*